P9-DWE-930

THE SUNBIRD

Books by Elizabeth E. Wein

THE WINTER PRINCE

A COALITION OF LIONS

THE SUNBIRD

THE SUNBIRD

ELIZABETH E. WEIN

VIKING

VIKING
Published by Penguin Group
Penguin Young Readers Group, 345 Hudson Street, New York, New York 10014, U.S.A.
Penguin Books Ltd, 80 Strand, London WC2R 0RL, England
Penguin Books Australia Ltd, 250 Camberwell Road, Camberwell, Victoria 3124, Australia
Penguin Books Canada Ltd, 10 Alcorn Avenue, Toronto, Ontario, Canada M4V 3B2
Penguin Books (N.Z.) Ltd, 182-190 Wairau Road, Auckland 10, New Zealand

First published in 2004 by Viking, a division of Penguin Young Readers Group

1 3 5 7 9 10 8 6 4 2

LIBRARY OF CONGRESS CATALOGING-IN-PUBLICATION DATA
Wein, Elizabeth.
The sunbird / by Elizabeth E. Wein.
p. cm.
Sequel to: A coalition of lions.
Summary: When, in the sixth century, plague spreads from Britain to Aksum, young Telemakos travels to the kingdom's salt mines to discover the identity of the traitor to the crown who, ignoring the emperor's command, is spreading plague with the salt from port to port.
ISBN 0-670-03691-9 (HARDCOVER)
[1. Plague—Fiction. 2. Aksum (Kingdom)—Fiction. 3. Salt mines and mining—Fiction.] I. Title.
PZ7.W4358Su 2004
[Fic]—dc22
2003017372

Printed in U.S.A.
Set in Goudy

For Sara

Launch out on his story, Muse, daughter of Zeus,
start from where you will—sing for our time too.

Homer, The Odyssey *1:11–12*

BOUNDARIES MARKING JUSTINIANIC PLAGUE

A.D. 541 AND AFTER

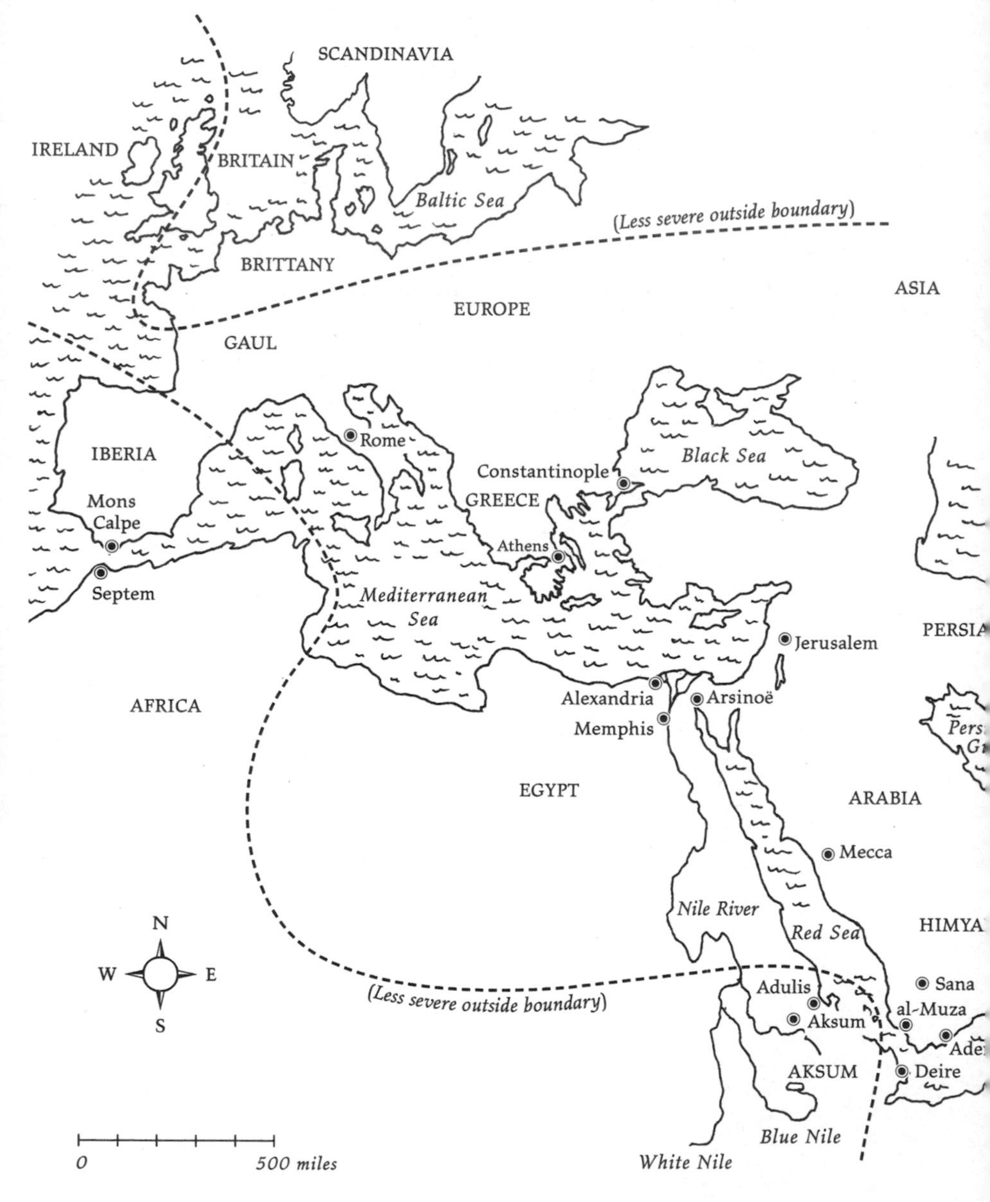

KINGDOM OF AKSUM

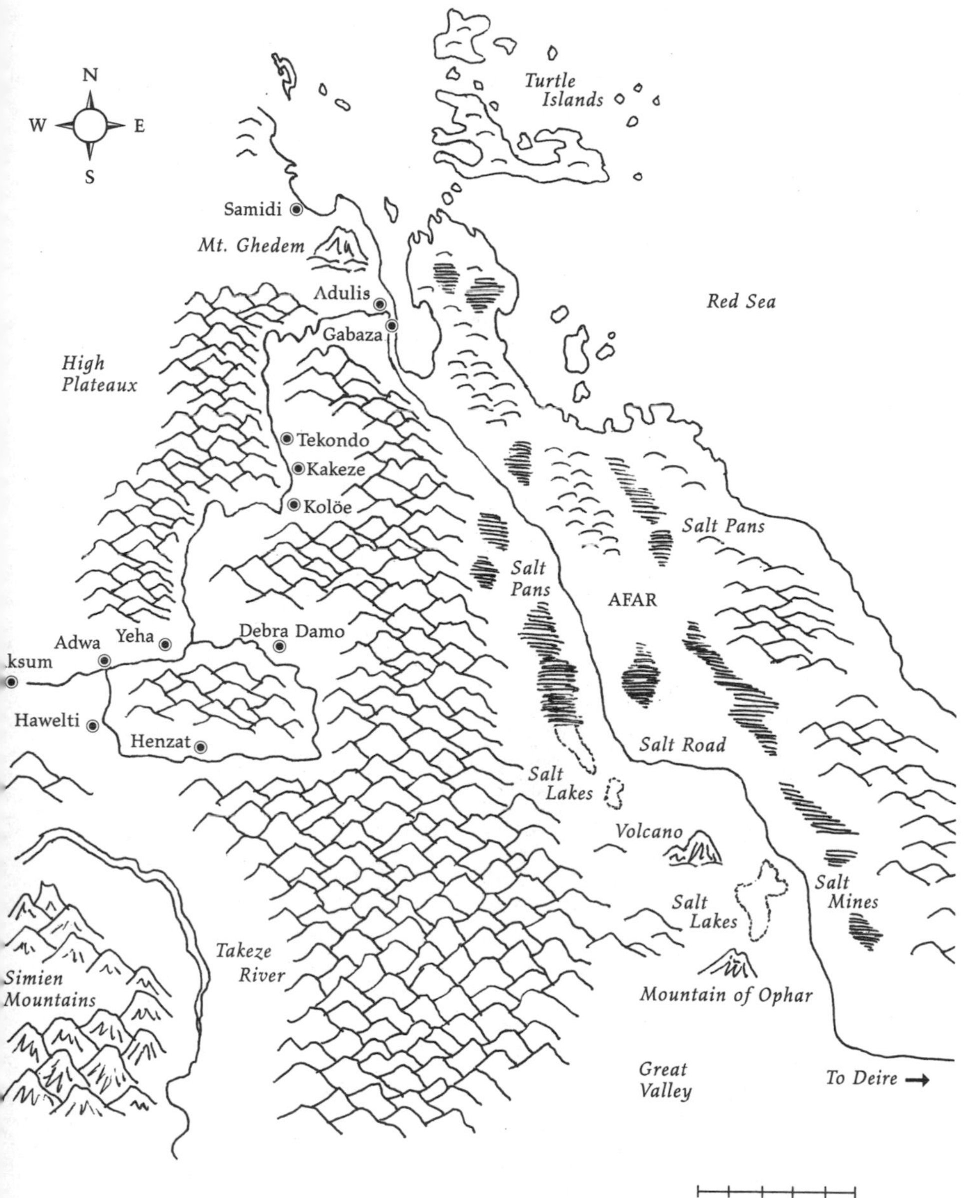

CONTENTS

I. *The Salt Traders* 1

II. *Invisible People* 15

III. *The Caracal* 26

IV. *Doves for the Poor* 43

V. *In the Lion's Den* 57

VI. *Goewin and Her Brothers* 72

VII. *A Dogfight* 83

VIII. *Abraham and Isaac* 93

IX. *Telemakos Alone* 109

X. The *Lazarus* 125

XI. *Light and Water* 134

XII. *Santaraj* 151

XIII. *The Harrier Stricken* 164

XIV. *Odysseus Bends His Bow* 173

Family Tree 186

Glossary 188

THE SUNBIRD

THE SALT TRADERS

Ready Telemachus took her up at once.
The Odyssey, *1:267–68*

TELEMAKOS WAS HIDING in the New Palace. He lay among the palms at the edge of the big fountain in the Golden Court. The marble lip of the fountain's rim just cleared the top of his head, and the imported soil beneath his chest was warm and moist. He was comfortable. He could move about easily behind the plants, for the sound of the fountains hid any noise he might make. Telemakos was watching his aunt.

She, Goewin, ought rightfully to be queen of Britain, queen of kings in her own land. Everyone said this. But she had chosen to send her cousin, Constantine, home to Britain as its high king, and she had taken his place here in African Aksum as Britain's ambassador. Goewin was young, barely a dozen years older than Telemakos himself. She often held informal audiences in unofficial places, like the Golden Court. She said she liked the sound of the fountains. Telemakos sometimes lay in his hiding place for hours, listening, listening. He did not understand all he heard, nor did he talk about it. But he loved to listen.

These men were not taking his aunt seriously, Telemakos could tell. They were talking about the salt trade. One of them was an official from Deire, in the far south beyond the Salt Desert, and one was a merchant, and one was a chieftain from Afar, where the valuable amole salt blocks were cut. The men were supposed to be negotiating a way of sending a regular salt shipment to Britain in exchange for tin and wool. But their conversation had deteriorated into a litany of complaints, and they spoke to one another without acknowledging Goewin's presence, as if she were a servant or an interpreter. If they did acknowledge her, it was to make some condescending explanation, as though she were a child.

Telemakos knew how this felt. It was one reason he had become adept at keeping himself hidden. People taunted him for his British father's hair, or they touched it superstitiously as if it would bring them luck; it was so fair as to be nearly white, incongruously framing a fine-drawn Aksumite face the color of coffee. And everyone hated his stony blue eyes, for which he could not blame them. "Foreign One" was the least offensive name they gave him. It was something Telemakos had lived with all his life, and he thought he did not mind it. But it was not something to which his aunt was accustomed, and he knew that it made her angry.

She dismissed the party of merchants and officials. They were listening with enough of an ear to her that they heard her dismissal.

Goewin sat for a moment in the quiet court then, empty of all life except the bright fish that darted through the water around the fountain. She drew a long breath, not so much a sigh as the noise she might have made before steeling herself to tease out a splinter of glass lodged in the palm of her hand. Then she said suddenly, "Telemakos, come here."

He had never been found out before, by anyone.

He was so surprised that for a long moment he did not move or answer her, expecting her command to have been a mistake, or believing himself to be dreaming.

"Telemakos," Goewin said, in a voice of dreadful imperial frost that brooked no argument, "I will not be disobeyed by you."

Telemakos crawled out from among the palms, silently, and knelt before his aunt with his head bowed.

"Do you make some use of your practiced espionage," she said. "Follow that party of dissembling tricksters and see if you can discover what tiresome plot they were hiding from me so carefully."

"Lady?" Telemakos asked tentatively, not sure that she could be serious, or why she was not angry with him.

"Follow them," said Goewin, "and listen."

So he did.

He stalked them like a leopard through the halls of the palace, gauging their attention, and watching the interaction of their servants even more closely than he watched the men themselves. They had a large number of attendants among them, from porters carrying sample bars of salt to children looking after exotic pets. The Deire official had a huge black cat on a lead. It was muzzled, and the merchant's clutch of half a dozen tiny monkeys were making it crazy. A tall boy with a thin moustache hung on to the cat's lead; four boys of about Telemakos's age seemed to be in charge of the miniature monkeys.

Telemakos, their shadow behind benches and pillars and potted trees, could not hear what they were saying. He needed to be with the party to hear them. Before he could frighten himself with the possible consequences, he slung a pebble at the leg of one of the monkeys.

He did not like to do it. But he did not trust people to react as predictably as animals. He would rather have dealt with the cat than the monkey, but there were four boys of varying shades and ages in the monkey retinue, and only the one older boy in charge of the cat. Telemakos needed to pass unnoticed.

His marksman father had never managed to sharpen Telemakos's aim, and it took Telemakos three quick shots before he struck his mark. Then there was a little explosion of temper and chaos as the monkey whirled and screamed and tried to bite back, striking out at the unfortunate child who held its lead. Telemakos ran up to the monkey, caught it by the scruff of its neck, and shook it. He gentled it while running with the other boys, who were all leaping to still the eruption and not draw attention to themselves from their masters. Telemakos stepped aside so that it looked to the monkey band as though he had momentarily crossed over from the cat band, and the haughty cat boy paid him no attention because Telemakos was obviously with the monkeys.

There was a moment, then, when he realized with a thrill through the pit of his stomach as though he were swooping from the boundary wall to the roof of his grandfather's stables, that he was standing in plain sight of twenty people and no one saw him.

The worst that could happen was that he would be chased off or reported to his grandfather, Kidane, who sat on the emperor's council. And his grandfather would not punish him. He would scold him, perhaps, but he would assume that Telemakos had been attracted to the cat, which was almost true. The roaring in Telemakos's head quieted, and he began to listen.

They spoke in Greek, and Telemakos could understand it, because it was the common language of the Red Sea. At least, he could understand the words they said, but he doubted their meaning. The men did not trust one another, and Telemakos's Greek was imperfect. He paid as much attention as he could to the sound of the words, so that he could repeat them accurately.

Cutting himself away from the group was even simpler than joining it had been. The owner of the fabulous cat suddenly turned around and snapped at his animal keeper in an incomprehensible language: "Go feed that creature!" or more likely, "Get that stinking feline away from us!"—the big cat smelled very strongly of big cat, and must have been intolerable when it was in heat. The thin moustache headed off in a different direction, pulling the cat with him. Telemakos peeled away from the party with the cat, and left its haughty keeper before he bothered to look down his long nose at the strange boy trotting at his heels.

Telemakos hugged himself into a granite alcove and stood still there for a moment, breathing lightly and trying to calm the roaring that had surged again in his ears. With most of his mind he dutifully repeated the words he needed to recite to his aunt; but with a small, delighted portion of himself he whispered aloud his new talent:

"I am invisible."

"Are you sure that is what he said?"

Goewin did not doubt that Telemakos was repeating to her what he thought he had heard. But she doubted that he could have heard it.

"'Plague will raise the price of salt,'" repeated Telemakos.

"There is no plague."

"That is what the Afar said. And the official from Deire—Anako?—Anako said that it had spread from Asia along the trade routes into Egypt, and across Europe as far as Britain and Byzantium to east and west, and that no one cared to buy cloth or spice or grain in any Mediterranean port, but wine and salt were dearly sought and dearly bought."

Goewin drew Telemakos down to sit by her on the fountain's rim.

"And what more did you hear?" she asked slowly.

"Alexandria . . . Alexandria? Where the abuna, the bishop, comes from. Alexandria is considering a—a curfew? They used a different word, but I think that is what they meant. No ships allowed in or out. And the merchant said that if there were such a law passed, it would make no difference to the African and Asian traders on the Red Sea, because they would take their goods to Arsinoë and sell them there for a dearer price. It wasn't curfew—"

"It was quarantine," said Goewin. "Quarantine."

She put an arm around his shoulders and hugged him against her. "You are a bold hero. I have told you that before."

He longed to look into her face, so pale and foreign and stern, but it would have been rude. Goewin sometimes commanded him to look at her, when she wanted his attention, but he did not dare to do it without her permission.

"Go on, then." Goewin tilted her head in the direction of the Golden Court's portal. "Go lose yourself. I've got another meeting in a minute, and I don't need you lurking at my feet."

Telemakos wandered through the busy halls of the New Palace and out to the lion pit. The emperor's lions were dozing in the shade of the young pencil cedars. Telemakos climbed down the keeper's rope.

"Hey, hey, hey, Sheba, you big bully. Get away from my feet."

Telemakos landed lightly in the grass at the foot of the pit. Sheba, the lioness, buffeted her great golden head against his; Solomon, the magnificent black-maned lion, yawned and did not move from his spot beneath the trees.

"La, my lovely, I'm glad to see you, too." Telemakos buried his face in Sheba's sun-heated fur. She smelled like frankincense. "What have you been rolling in, you pampered creature? What a waste of good spice!"

The lions' bodies belonged to the emperor, but their hearts belonged to Telemakos. He had captured them himself, as kits, and given them as a coronation gift to Wazeb, now the emperor Gebre Meskal, negusa nagast, the king of kings of the Aksumite peoples. By day they lived in the lion pit of the New Palace. They wandered freely over the grounds at night, too fat and lazy to bother the pet elephant and giraffe that wandered there also, but daunting enough to any would-be thief or assassin. Telemakos was no more in awe of them now than he had been when he plucked them, small and golden-spotted and squirming, from the nest of rocks where their aunties had left them while they went hunting.

He liked to play with the lions when his mind was empty, and to snuggle with them in the sun when he had something to think about.

Plague in Britain was what he was thinking about now. He had never been to Britain, but he felt connected to it, living daily with his British aunt. Telemakos shared Goewin's rejoicing when packets arrived from Ras Priamos, the emperor's cousin, Aksum's ambassador to Britain. It was four years since they had seen each other, but Goewin's heart was in her homeland with the Aksumite envoy, Telemakos knew; he knew how she treasured Priamos's letters, how devotedly she answered them. If plague was in Britain, Priamos might be lost to her; and if plague was in Britain, Telemakos was sure his father would never take him there.

But if it had spread through Egypt already, then might it not end in Aksum itself, and who would then waste time worrying about distant Britain?

Goewin will tell the emperor, Telemakos thought, if I know Goewin. She'll tell him this afternoon, because there's a meeting of the bala heg this afternoon; that's why Grandfather came up to the New Palace this morning. He never comes up here unless the council is meeting.

Lying in the sun with his face against Sheba's spicy fur, Telemakos conceived an intrigue so elaborate it verged on folly.

He contrived to gain entry to that afternoon's meeting of the bala heg, the parliament of twelve nobles who gave private counsel to the young emperor Gebre Meskal. Telemakos hid himself in plain sight, just as he had done with the salt traders. This time he made Grandfather believe that he was attending the council as Goewin's unlikely companion, and he made her believe that he was there with Grandfather.

Telemakos walked between them as they entered the council room, his head held high, his eyes on the floor. He could sense Kidane and Goewin glaring at each other accusingly, not daring to start a personal argument in the emperor's presence. Telemakos kept his gaze trained on the floor. He bowed to the emperor with Kidane and Goewin, lower than either of them because he was younger and had no place here.

He lay on his chest on the floor with his face in his arms until Gebre Meskal acknowledged him.

"Lij Telemakos."

That sobered him. It was very rare that anyone called him by his title, which was something equivalent to "young prince." Telemakos's mother and grandfather only ever introduced him as Telemakos Meder, his own name and his father's Aksumite name. Yet his mother was a noble and his father a prince, and though Telemakos was Aksumite by birth, by blood he had more claim to the British kingship than did Constantine, Britain's high king.

For one uncertain moment Telemakos feared the emperor would ask why he was there. Then Gebre Meskal said, as though in warning, "All right, Telemakos," speaking in tones of dismissal.

Telemakos stood up, his eyes still trained on the floor. He moved to stand aside with his face to the wall, to show how well he knew his place; he was sure that this was a courtesy Grandfather would have required of him if he had truly brought him to this meeting.

Gebre Meskal acknowledged his councilors with no more of a greeting than he had given to Telemakos, and called for their silence.

"Princess." Gebre Meskal was always as respectful to Goewin as he was to anyone, and it was partly this that kept Telemakos in awe of her. "You have news from our ambassador in Britain?"

"Thank you for allowing me entry here today, Your

Majesty," Goewin said coolly. "Yes, only this noon I've received a letter from Priamos."

"I await my own," said the emperor. "The despatchers are erratic as ever."

"There may be good reason for that," said Goewin. "May I read this aloud?"

And there it was again, the evil word, *plague*. Priamos's letter confirmed that it was in Britain. Priamos apologized that he would not return to Aksum that year, as planned and expected, because he did not think it safe to travel. He also advised that Goewin stay where she was: "For to move from one land to another is to drag the pestilence from place to place, and to leave a wake of death and uncleanness in one's path."

There was a long silence after Goewin finished.

She spoke grimly, into the heavy silence, "I am going to write one more letter to Constantine the high king, and tell him to shut down Britain's ports. And I entreat you, Your Majesty, to do the same here in Aksum."

The council chamber exploded into outrage. Telemakos turned his head, very quietly and carefully, so that he could see over one shoulder a little of what was going on.

There was old Zoskales, who was deaf and always asleep, starting and blinking; his neighbor, Karkara, yelled an explanation at his ear. The warrior Hiuna and the priest Kasu, from the ancient city of Yeha, had broken into angry argument with each other; while Ityopis, the emperor's young cousin, slapped the rail before them with one open palm to try to calm them or get their attention.

Telemakos found himself shaking with bottled laughter. Each one of the bala heg was behaving exactly as he did in court or in the street. Telemakos could not believe they were so predictable.

Goewin leaned an elbow against the rail in front of her own seat, her head tilted a little, her eyes hidden behind one hand. She waited in disgusted silence for the council to come to order. Telemakos moved his head imperceptibly, straining to get a better look, and found Goewin watching him from beneath her hand. She held his gaze for a moment before he could duck back toward the wall. His heart hammered; he was sure she had discovered him again.

Well, there was no doubt Grandfather would have him whipped this time, for this was the most outrageous thing he had ever done. But he would not give himself up until he was called out.

It was Danael who brought them to order. He was their leader, the agabe heg, the king's closest advisor.

"Have you so little regard for the British ambassador?" he thundered. "Sit down. Would you question Caleb's choice of her any more than you question his choice of Gebre Meskal as his heir? Sit down and be quiet and let her speak."

Danael turned to the negusa nagast. "Your Majesty?"

"Come to your feet, Princess Goewin, and address them again," said the emperor.

Telemakos heard her stand up. She said simply, "Close your ports. Close your borders. You will lose commerce, you will lose authority, you will lose alliances. But you have the strength to do it and survive. The world is aflame. If you would live through this scourge, you must cut yourself off from the world."

A few of the council sent up a murmur of assent. Telemakos heard Grandfather's voice among them. Zoskales muttered something, loudly but incomprehensibly, in his flat, hissing voice.

"'What is the child doing here?'" Karkara repeated clearly.

Telemakos drew in a sharp breath.

"Turn around, Telemakos," said Goewin.

He turned to face them, staring at his feet.

"I asked him here as my witness," said Goewin smoothly. "He was with me this morning when I first heard rumor of the plague, from Anako, the archon in Deire. And it was in conversation with Anako's porters that Telemakos heard speculation as to how to undermine the quarantine in Alexandria. Where there is no market, there will be a black market. So I would advise you not only to set quarantine in your own land, but also to lay careful snares against any who would slip through your net."

Now, though he was still gazing studiously at the floor, Telemakos knew they were all staring at him. The emperor said, "Tell us what was spoken, child."

Telemakos answered dutifully.

"You are speaking Ethiopic," said Gebre Meskal. "Is that what you heard?"

"They were speaking Greek," Telemakos corrected himself, and carefully repeated the salt traders' words as accurately as he could, as though he were reciting a language lesson.

"You heard this in conversation with Anako's *porters?*" questioned Karkara.

"Not exactly; it was not the porters speaking, sir," Telemakos said. "Anako and the Afar chieftain were talking to each other. I was with the porters, looking at their animals."

Another great murmur breathed through the chamber as the bala heg considered.

"When do you envision this quarantine enacted?" Gebre Meskal asked Goewin.

"Tomorrow," she said.

Invisible People

The goddess swept into the cavern's shadowed vault,
searching for hiding-places far inside its depths . . .
13:418–19

HAVING PLAYED HIS part, Telemakos stood listening quietly, his face to the wall, until the council was finished.

He walked between his grandfather and his aunt again as they filed out of the private chamber and into the busy reception hall. There a typical drama was being enacted as the youngest of the emperor's cousins, twin girls who were some two or three years older than Telemakos, fought with each other. Telemakos sometimes thought he had never spent a day in the New Palace when he had not come across the simple-minded daughters of Candake, queen of queens, negeshta nagashtat, raising their voices in anger against each other. He avoided them whenever possible, as did everyone else.

Only now he kept track of them out of the corner of his eye, as a means of escape.

Grandfather turned on Goewin as soon as they were through the door of the council chamber, and Goewin in turn snatched hold of Telemakos by the shoulder lest he, predictably, disappear.

"Never again!" Grandfather said, and it occurred to Telemakos that he had not ever known Kidane to be angry with Goewin. "Never again, without consulting me first! The boy is my grandson. What will they think of me in this court, dragging children into the emperor's private councils! That I should bring such shame upon the noble house of Nebir!"

Goewin knelt before Kidane, her head bowed. She had released Telemakos, but he stayed by her side out of loyalty, since she was now his conspirator.

"Blatte Kidane, Councilor Kidane, forgive me. I most humbly beg your pardon. I would not bring shame on my host and patron. I thought there could be no blame on any but myself. And I will take all blame on myself."

Telemakos knelt also.

"And as for you, my boy—" Grandfather began, but Goewin cut him off.

"The blame is all mine," she repeated. "Do not find fault in him for obeying me."

Kidane stood for a moment, nonplussed, while Goewin demeaned herself. Telemakos felt his heart fluttering, torn between exultation at having escaped his grandfather's wrath, and apprehension at what form his aunt's would take.

Kidane raised Goewin to her feet and kissed her on either cheek. They liked and respected each other, and this scene was embarrassing to both of them. "I see why you would do such a thing," Grandfather said. "But I beg you, Princess, do not surprise me like this again."

"I will not," said Goewin meaningfully.

Then a reluctant page came forward to relay the message to Goewin that her salt merchants were awaiting their unfinished audience with her, as she had arranged. Did she indeed mean to meet with them that day, or had she forgotten them?

Telemakos watched her face cloud with anger and irritation.

"I'll be there. I am there now."

She pulled her shamma shawl into place across her shoulders, and turned briefly to Telemakos. "Come to me in the Golden Court, you, in an hour."

"Yes, my lady."

She went with the page. Before Kidane could scold his grandson anyway, Telemakos slipped away into the strange, charmed company of the simple-minded princesses, whom everyone ignored.

They were always dressed exactly alike. Their hair was always plaited in the exact same way, with the exact same gold and emerald beads threaded through it. As far as he could tell, their battles were caused mostly by one of them trying to get away from the other, and the abandoned one following and weeping.

"You be quiet," he told them. "The emperor is coming through in a minute."

"The emperor is my cousin," said one of them. "Don't tell

me how to behave in his presence, you freakish little crossbred snoop."

Telemakos gaped. The last thing he expected to hear from them was an apt and vicious insult. They were supposed to be stupid.

"You should bow before you speak to us," said the other, nodding vigorously, backing her sister.

"Don't bother," said the first. "No one does anything Esato tells them. Esato's a baby."

"*You* are a baby," said Esato.

Telemakos looked at them and saw for the first time that they were not identical. They were not even alike. They were identically dressed and ornamented, indeed, as if they were a broken plate that someone had tried to glue back together and pass off as whole. But Esato was simple, and Sofya was not. It was obvious, if you bothered to look at them.

"Oh, shut your mouth, boy," said Sofya. "You look like a fish. We're the numbwits, not you."

"Shut your mouth," Esato echoed.

"Sorry," Telemakos said.

"Why in the world are you talking to us?" Sofya walked quickly away from the press around the council room doorway, and Telemakos went with her. Esato, too, followed, one hand clinging to a fold of Sofya's skirt, while Sofya angrily but absently tried to disengage her.

"Because no one sees you," said Telemakos honestly. "I'm escaping my grandfather. He's Kidane, one of the bala heg."

Sofya laughed aloud, and a fraction of a second later, following her sister's lead like an obedient puppy, Esato laughed also. "Truly?" Sofya said. "Yes," she continued, "truly, I can see it, because you would never have bothered otherwise. Well, come on, then. Let's hide you somewhere. Esato, we must rescue him from the evil bala heg, do you see?"

"Take him to Our Mother," said Esato.

"Yes, he's a favorite with the queen of queens, aren't you, you slinking little mountain jackal? She likes your grotesque hair. But let's not go to Our Mother, they'll all think to look for him there. Somewhere else . . ."

Esato stopped pulling at her sister's dress, happy to be part of this new conspiracy. She took Telemakos by one hand. Sofya took him by the other.

Telemakos was led through parts of the New Palace that he had never seen; for well as he knew it, he did not live there, and had no real place there. The twins pulled him outside, and they passed armories and butteries and a jeweler's workshop, all loosely strung out along an awned walkway beyond the main building of the palace itself. At last they came to a pair of granite platforms, each patrolled by pairs of spearmen. There were wide stairways leading to the tops of the platforms and, below them, heavy doors guarding a space beneath the ground. Sofya stopped before one of these doors and hailed a sentry.

"You can't go in there!" Telemakos said. "That's the emperor's treasury!"

"We go anywhere we like," said Esato.

"We're stupid, you see," said Sofya. "We would never take

anything." She gave Telemakos a sidelong glance. "Whereas you, little mountain jackal, will be searched before they let you out again."

A guard loped down the platform stairs, his expression caught between amusement and mild irritation. He pushed back the bars on one of the heavy doors for them.

"Do you want a light, Woyzaro Sofya, Princess?" he asked.

"Just leave the door open," Sofya said. "Coming in, are you, Telemakos Meder? Or shall you go back to your grandfather?"

Telemakos followed the girls down the massive granite stairs and into the underground vaults.

The great entrance hall was lit well by sunlight from the open doorway. The rooms that flanked the hall loomed darker, but the whole was strangely luminous once your eyes adjusted to the gloom. Telemakos's first impression was that the odd light came from the walls. Then he saw that the hall and the chambers beyond it were stacked nearly to their high ceilings with blocks and blocks of what appeared to be white stone: marble, quartz? It sparkled faintly when it caught the light. In the narrow aisles between the great white stacks he saw gold and pearls and other riches, sorted in trays and coffers, but these seemed incidental. The glittering towers of cut stone overshadowed everything else.

"What is this?" Telemakos asked.

"This side is gold from the northern provinces."

"I mean, what is *this*?" He laid the edge of a hand against one of the coldly gleaming bars.

"Salt, you cretin. What else would it be?"

The emperor's treasury was filled from wall to wall with amole, the bars of cut salt that passed for currency wherever gold was scarce.

"Don't touch it," Sofya said. "You'll stain it."

"Don't touch," Esato echoed, and struck his hand aside with startling speed and strength. The rough salt grazed his wrist bone hard enough to draw blood, and he yelped.

"Do you be careful, Esato," her sister hissed. "They will make us leave." Then to Telemakos she added, "You'll be whipped if you mar the salt. Keep your hands to yourself."

Sofya continued to lead him through the salt maze. Telemakos sucked at his stinging wrist. He followed silently, tasting blood and salt. It was without a doubt the most sinister place he had ever been. He did not like it.

"Where are we going?" he asked.

"We've got our own strongbox. We're allowed to look at the things, and try them on. Esato likes to pretend she's getting married."

There was scarcely any light in the corner of the vault where the princesses' coffer was. The strangeness of it all was beginning to make Telemakos nervous. It was cold out of the sun, under the ground, and he pulled his shamma tightly around his shoulders. He stood hugging his arms over his chest as he watched the girls playacting a strange ritual, in which Sofya adorned her sister as a bride, or a doll. Telemakos noticed that Sofya did not once try any of the ornaments on herself. Esato remained passive, but as the game went on she seemed to become curiously radiant, her odd, wide features serene, her hair and throat and arms lightly glittering with precious stone and precious metal. It made Telemakos feel faintly sad.

"Lovely Esato," he said aloud. "You're beautiful now."

They both stared at him as if they had completely forgotten he was there.

Esato said wisely, "Look: the little mountain jackal doesn't like it here."

Sofya sighed. "Come on, then. Put the things back."

They led Telemakos again through the towers of salt, and he saw his way out; the stairway to the sun filled him with an absurd well of relief.

"Wait," Sofya said, and put out a hand to bar his way. She called out loudly, "Watchman!"

The silhouette of the guard appeared at the top of the stair, blocking the entrance. "Princess?"

"We're coming out now. Will you search this boy?"

She knew perfectly well that Telemakos had not touched a thing except the bars of salt when they first came in, and he considered arguing; but common sense told him this was palace protocol, something he must endure whether or not it was fair. He stood his ground and waited for the man to come down the stairway.

"Clothes off, boy."

Telemakos hesitated, frowning, but the man was three times his size and stood between him and his way out. Telemakos peeled off his shamma and shirt.

"Kilt. Sandals."

He stripped in sullen silence. Esato tittered.

"Turn around: bend over."

This was a bit much.

"I haven't taken anything!" Telemakos snarled. But he obeyed.

"Indeed you have not," laughed the guard. He picked up Telemakos's clothes and herded the three children ahead of him up the stairs. At the top there was a chorus of chuckles from the rest of the patrol as Telemakos emerged. He tried to imagine his formidable father coerced like this, and decided it was possible to behave with dignity even if you were naked. Chieftains undressed to the waist when they came to beg audiences with the emperor; their humility did not diminish their nobility. When the watchman tossed the boy's clothes at his feet, Telemakos knelt and carefully strapped on his sandals as if he did not care who was looking at him. He held his back straight and head high; the sun lit his bare shoulders with warmth.

"Will you come talk to us another time?" asked Sofya, as Telemakos stood up, adjusting his shamma.

"Not if you make me undress again," Telemakos answered sharply, and walked away from them. Goewin would by now be waiting for him in the Golden Court, and Sofya and Esato could follow if they wanted. But they did not.

Goewin was indeed waiting for him. She was writing, sitting on the floor at the fountain's edge, so that the wide marble rim served as her table. She was another who could maintain her dignity no matter what she did.

Telemakos would have bowed, but it was impossible to abase himself before her when she was sitting on the ground. He stood silently and waited for her to acknowledge him.

At last Goewin looked up. "Well, Telemakos?"

It was like being questioned by the Sphinx; you prayed she was not about to devour you.

He knelt swiftly at her side, grasped her hand, and kissed it lightly. "I owe you a thousand apologies—"

"You owe me a debt of gratitude," said Goewin. Her loved voice was frost hard, and cold. "If you ever do that again—" She was as powerful and dangerous as her elder half brother, Medraut, Telemakos's father, whom the Aksumites had named Ras Meder, Prince Meder. "If you ever do that again, don't let anyone see you."

It was not the threat he had been expecting.

"Do you understand me?"

Telemakos began a new apology. "I am a thousand times sorry—"

"Stop. Don't feign sweet innocence like that, you are too charming. Listen again," Goewin said. "I have a message for you from the emperor. He says to tell you this. When you can prove to him you have sat through a meeting of the bala heg without any of them knowing it, he will make you his private emissary."

Telemakos held her hand tightly, staring at it, and Goewin squeezed his hand in return. "Look at me, Telemakos."

He tilted his head to look up into her face. She and her

half brother were the only adults he knew who ever demanded that he meet their gaze when they wanted to command his attention. Telemakos watched Goewin seriously. In her dark eyes he thought he saw the same fierce excitement that had driven him to attempt this venture himself.

Goewin said, "We mean this, Telemakos."

THE CARACAL

Down over the rugged road they went till hard by town
they reached the stone-rimmed fountain running clear
where the city people came and drew their water.
17:222–24

A FAINT SCENT of sweat and frankincense woke Telemakos in the still, quiet midnight of his grandfather's mansion, and made him sure that his father was home.

His father was never to be found when you looked for him. Medraut stayed away for weeks at a time hunting with the royal elephant herders, or hunting on his own; and if he was not in the Simien Mountains or the Great Valley, he spent his days sequestered in Abba Pantelewon, the monastery set in the hills above the city. When Medraut was at home—Telemakos was not sure his father considered Kidane's house home, but that was where his wife and son lived—if Medraut was at home, he never said anything. Telemakos had never heard his father speak a single word aloud, except on one solitary, memorable occasion, when Medraut had cried out a warning, and had spoken his son's name.

Telemakos was rather proud to be named for Odysseus's son, though it was not lost on him that his name was his patient mother's subtle reprimand to his wayward father. Medraut had been in Britain when Telemakos was born, and had not known of his son's existence for the first six years of Telemakos's life. Having Medraut as a father was much like having Odysseus as a father, Telemakos thought, and he sympathized deeply with his namesake. There seemed only a slender difference between not knowing if your father was alive and never hearing his voice. The best part of *The Odyssey*, Telemakos thought, was the contest at the end, where Odysseus reveals himself by stringing his own bow, which no one else can do, although Telemakos nearly manages it; and then together they destroy the men who have been laying waste to their estate and plotting Telemakos's murder. How wonderful to be in league with your father like that, after nearly twenty years of hoping he was not already dead.

Telemakos climbed out of his own bed and felt his way through the sleeping house, as sure-footed and confident as if he were blind and always found his way by touch and smell and echo. As he had guessed, his mother was not alone in her bed. Telemakos wriggled in between his parents and pulled the blankets over him.

"Oh, *not you*, boy," said Turunesh sleepily, because she was as jealous of his father's attention as Telemakos, and had him to herself even less. She made room for Telemakos.

Telemakos lay still between his mother and father, savoring this moment when they were all three together and content, complete.

He dreamed that the lions were pretending to eat him. He was not afraid of them; he knew they were only playing. They took turns biting the top of his head. Their teeth closed tightly enough to sting his scalp, but not enough to break the skin. They were persistent, and Telemakos was beginning to be annoyed with the game, but he did not know how to get away from their teeth without hurting himself.

He woke, then; it was still dark. His parents were asleep. His scalp prickled. Telemakos reached up to touch his head and found his father's hand tangled in his hair.

He tried to unthread the taut, strong fingers, but his hair was nearly as thick as his mother's, and matted easily. It was a trial to Turunesh to keep it free of snarls. She liked it long, because it was so bright and so unusual and so like Medraut's. Medraut had a firm handful, and his grip was like iron. When Telemakos tried to free himself, Medraut sighed in his sleep and tightened his hold so fiercely that Telemakos could not move his head.

"Ah, little bright one," said Medraut in Latin, speaking low and clear. "What are you doing here?"

Telemakos lay frozen, his head trapped, so startled he was almost alarmed. Except for the shouted warning, Telemakos had never heard his father speak.

"Ras Meder?" he whispered, but he knew that Medraut was asleep, or he would not be talking. Telemakos spoke aloud. "Sir?"

Is he talking to *me*? Telemakos wondered, torn between delight and dread. *Little one*, he said, he must mean me. It did not strike Telemakos strange that Medraut spoke Latin, for it was still spoken throughout Britain, he knew, and Turunesh encouraged her half-British son to use it himself.

Medraut sighed again, his fingers still wound tight in Telemakos's hair. Then he uttered a string of syllables in no language Telemakos had ever heard.

It was like being brushed across the back of the neck: it made his arms break out in gooseflesh. Telemakos was tempted to wake Medraut, only to have his familiar silent self back, and not this gibberish-spouting night creature. But Telemakos wanted to hear the voice again. When Medraut had shouted his son's name, it had been a terrible sound of fear and warning. This was his real voice, low and deep and gentle, full of music.

Telemakos reached up once more to touch his father's hand. Medraut spoke the same string of nonsense, the same sequence. Telemakos listened with all his being, trying to hold the shape of the sound in his mind. He mouthed the syllables over to himself so that he would remember them, as he had done with the words of the salt traders. Telemakos felt sure that whatever language his father spoke in his sleep, his aunt could interpret.

He lay awake and tense for a long time after that, his head imprisoned, repeating the impossible sentence and straining to hear anything else. But Medraut did not speak again. Telemakos did fall asleep at last, because when next he tried to move his head it was free, and the bright dawn was sneaking into the room, and he and his mother were alone in her bed.

Telemakos found Goewin packing her ambassador's satchel. It was still early morning.

"Have you got anything exciting in there today?" Telemakos asked. She had once brought home a live cricket in a tiny house of carven ivory.

"Here are little amole," Goewin said, and gave him a handful of miniature tablets of salt. "Pretty, aren't they?"

"What are they for?"

"Money. Or soup."

Telemakos laughed. "'A rich man eats salt,'" he said, quoting his grandfather. He gave the tablets back to Goewin. "What does this mean?" he asked, and repeated what he had heard Medraut say.

Goewin packed the salt back in her bag and put it down. Then she stared at Telemakos. She did not answer, so he said it again.

"Where did you hear that?"

"Ras Meder said it in his sleep."

Goewin had been startled when Telemakos repeated Medraut's strange words, but she did not seem surprised when he told her his source. "Medraut has always talked in his sleep," she said. "It's why he usually spends the night in a hermit's hole halfway up the cliff wall at Abba Pantelewon. He doesn't like anyone to hear him. He would give away state secrets in his sleep, if he had any."

"But what does it mean, what he said?"

"In my native dialect it means, 'Little brother, go back to bed.'" With bluff, sharp movements, Goewin stuffed maps and a stylus into her satchel.

Telemakos was perplexed. He frowned, and said, "What did he mean, *little brother*? Did he mean me?"

"Of course not," Goewin said shortly. "Did you go back to bed?"

"I didn't. . . . But I didn't understand."

"He wasn't talking to you," said Goewin, and flicked shut the brass clasps on her bag. "He thought you were someone else. He thought I was someone else once, too, and smacked me in the face. He's monstrous in his sleep. I don't know how your mother endures him."

"Who is Ras Meder's little brother?"

"He was my twin brother. His name was Lleu, the Bright One, the young lion. Lleu son of Artos. He was the prince of Britain; he should have been high king of Britain instead of Constantine, but he died in the battle of Camlan, just before I came here to Aksum. Goodness, Telemakos, you were there during all that fuss about making my cousin Constantine the new high king, you must have heard us speaking of Lleu. I thought you heard everything."

He did hear everything. He did know who Lleu was. Only he had never considered that the lost prince of Britain had been anyone's small brother: a young person not unlike himself, who might suddenly need affection when everyone else was asleep, and be lightly scolded for waking people.

"Why does Ras Meder still talk to Lleu in his sleep?"

"He loved Lleu more than anything. Lleu's death broke Medraut into pieces. I think it's why he won't talk to anyone.

"Coming with me this morning?" Goewin finished abruptly, shouldering her satchel. "Or is your father going to take you hunting?"

"He is," Telemakos answered forcefully, although this had not been established, or even hinted at, in his odd paternal encounter in the middle of the night. But it was the chief reason Medraut made his sudden appearances in Kidane's house, and it was what Telemakos lived for.

Medraut took Telemakos well out of the city when they hunted together. They might be gone for as long as a fortnight, often staying at Kidane's country estate at Adwa, so that Telemakos could be left in safe hands when Medraut sometimes went out on his own. On more than one occasion they had departed for Adwa without telling anyone where they were going or how long they would be gone, Telemakos because he did not know, and Medraut because he never told anyone anything; it did not occur to either one of them that Turunesh might want to know when her son was about to disappear for over a week. On this day Telemakos thought to warn her, and Turunesh gave him her blessing after a fashion:

"Oh, get gone. You are safer in the bush with Ras Meder than you are in the lion pit with Sheba and Solomon."

This was literally true, for Telemakos had once come home from the lion pit with a finger ripped through to the bone, while Medraut never brought him back with any hurt more serious than carefully tended briar scratches.

Their hunting together chiefly consisted of creeping noiselessly through savanna and slough, lying silent in long grass, waiting and watching. Medraut could come close enough to an unwary gazelle that he could snatch hold of it by its horns and the back of its neck, like a lion, while it rolled its eyes and tried to twist its head free. Medraut shot and threw with fearful accuracy, but Telemakos did not doubt that if Medraut wanted for meat he would need no tool other than his hands.

Telemakos was Medraut's equal as a tracker, and would soon be his better. His legs were not as long as his father's, so he was not as fast; but he was much smaller and even quieter, and he could smell things that Medraut could not.

No one had taught him this skill. It had come through long, long, silent hours of waiting and watching and listening. Telemakos knew lions so well that he could sometimes scent what they had eaten the day before. He could tell with fair accuracy, without looking, how long an animal had been dead. He could often tell what kind of antelope he was following before he saw it. He knew, at least a mile before they came to it, that today there was some wounded thing traveling ahead of them.

"Something's bleeding on the road," Telemakos said, to alert his father. "I don't know what. Everything stinks of baboon along here." Medraut nodded.

They did not necessarily expect to solve the mystery, since they were behind it. But after a time they came to a roadside well, shaded by giant sycamores, with a band of travelers crowded underneath the trees. Some were drinking at the well. At the edge of the band, a boy was being whipped. His bare back was scored with weals, raised though not bloody; he uttered a plaintive cry with each stroke. Medraut let his breath out sharply through his nostrils, a sound of disgust. Telemakos glanced up at his face. His father's dark blue eyes were narrowed in disapproval, hard and glittering as basalt.

"I still smell blood," Telemakos said, puzzled, though not as disturbed as his father.

Suddenly Medraut pulled Telemakos close against him with one arm like an iron band across his chest and the other hand clamped over his eyes like a blindfold.

"Hey!"

Telemakos struggled, pulling at the hand that was blinding him with both of his own, trying to pry it from his eyes. Medraut shifted his grip on his son and pulled one of Telemakos's arms behind his back.

Telemakos was outraged. "Let go! I have seen servants beaten before, I'm not a baby!"

Medraut gave a sharp, warning twist to Telemakos's imprisoned arm. Never before had he deliberately hurt his child. Telemakos went limp in his father's hold, shocked and betrayed. The heavy hand over his eyes held him blind.

The other child's pathetic, bleating cries carried on, and Telemakos could still smell blood, and something else out of the ordinary for a band of travelers: the sour reek of cat, which he had not been able to pick out on the road because of the baboons.

"Let me see," Telemakos begged. He did not mean that he wanted to watch; he only wanted not to be held blind like this. It was a violation. But Medraut held him close, gently while he did not move, more fiercely when he tried to break free. Medraut held Telemakos for as long as the wailing continued, and for a few more moments after it stopped. Then, keeping a heavy, guiding hand on the boy's shoulder, still warning, Medraut freed Telemakos's eyes and approached the knot of men who were grouped around the unfortunate servant child.

They were giving him a drink now, and pulling his shirt back over his head, a thing he could not do himself. Telemakos saw now that both the boy's hands had been cut off above the wrists. It could not have happened more than a day ago; one of the stumps still bled. That was the blood Telemakos had smelled. He suddenly understood why Medraut had not wanted him to witness the beating: not that it had itself been horrific, but that it was vile injustice inflicted on someone who was already enduring an incomprehensible suffering.

Medraut walked forward, Telemakos at his side. Telemakos glanced up at his father again, apprehensive. Medraut's narrowed eyes still burned coldly with disgust and disdain. He let go of his son's shoulder and held up his hand to the travelers, his open palm facing them as though in greeting. He stood so, impassive but for his accusing eyes, until two of them noticed him and came forward a little.

"What is that?" one asked.

"The staff of Asclepius. He is a physician."

Medraut held his open hand to Telemakos briefly, so that he could see what the others had seen. There was a blue tattoo on the palm of Medraut's left hand, a snake entwined about a branch.

Medraut was obviously foreign; his skin was so white you could pick him out in a crowd across the Cathedral Square. But merchants bargained wordlessly all the time, and because Medraut had approached with a gesture and not a word, the travelers assumed he could not speak, or did not speak their language. They talked between themselves as though they thought he could not hear, either. Telemakos marveled at their bland stupidity.

"What spleen, to think he will find work here!"

"Well, Butala does need that stump seen to."

"The master won't put out much for the doctoring of a faithless bond servant. See what the man will take as payment."

"I'm not paying him!"

The other rolled his eyes. "Mother of God. Only find out what he'll cost."

Medraut spat in the dust at their feet.

Telemakos said sharply, "He's not asking for payment, only for permission."

They looked at Telemakos in surprise, and then one of

them waved Medraut forward. "Please, do your worst."

Medraut turned to Telemakos and held up the blue serpent again. Then he pointed to the well in the center of the grove. He unslung his bow and quiver from his back and handed them to Telemakos.

"Could I help, though?" Telemakos offered.

Medraut pointed him away again, seriously, then turned his back on him. Telemakos went to sit by the well to wait for him.

There were three others on a stone bench there, two hunched tensely together in conversation, and one patently miserable with his head on his knees and his hands held tightly over his ears. At his feet lay a huge black cat with curling tufts of hair springing from its ears. Telemakos suddenly recognized them all, as though the trick to a puzzle box had just dawned on him and all the interlocking pieces made sense and fit together cleverly. This band was that of Anako, the archon from Deire, on his way home.

Telemakos said to the cowering boy, "Has the cat a name?"

It was the boy he had seen in the New Palace, with the thin moustache. He looked up at Telemakos without taking his hands from his ears. "What are you?" he asked disdainfully. "Why should I answer idle questions of someone else's servant?"

"I don't mind whether or not you speak to me," Telemakos said truthfully, not caring what they took him for. "I only wanted to look at the cat."

The boy let go of one of his ears so that he could reach

down to scratch the cat between its own fantastic ones.

"She's called Chariclea," the boy said. The cat was still muzzled. "Go ahead and touch her. She can't hurt you; she doesn't have any claws."

Telemakos knelt next to the cat. It looked as though it weighed nearly as much as he did; it was as big as a hunting dog. Telemakos ran both hands down its back. Its fur was sable silk.

"Is it a caracal? I thought only their ears were black."

"She's a black caracal. She's a freak, like you."

"I'm not a freak," said Telemakos mildly. He was so accustomed to this kind of jibe that he expected it. "I'm half-breed."

"You've the hair of an albino."

"I'm not albino. It's just light-colored. My father's hair looks like this."

"What's your father?"

"The doctor."

Telemakos glanced over his shoulder. Medraut had built a small fire and was kneeling over it, busy with something. Telemakos quickly looked away again. It would be bad enough having to listen, he knew, they all knew, without watching as well. He crouched low over the big cat's neck, raking gentle fingers through its exquisite fur. "Oh, you beauty, you lovely, you treasure!" he whispered to it.

The caracal stretched out its front legs blissfully, kneading at the ground. Its feet were toeless stumps, like hands with the fingers lopped off.

"Poor paws," said Telemakos.

"She doesn't care. She was never hurt, not much; they drugged her for the operation. Lucky old Chariclea. They didn't bother putting Butala to sleep."

"Ras Meder won't hurt him more than he has to," Telemakos said, an empty reassurance. He was fairly certain that Medraut was going to have to sear the boy's wounds to seal them, and that he did not have the time nor the herbs nor the equipment he needed to do it painlessly.

Telemakos and his sullen companion bore the worst of Butala's screaming each in his own way, the cat boy bent over with his head wrapped in his arms again, and Telemakos with his face buried against the caracal's side and his arms locked around its neck. When it was quiet again Telemakos raised his head, somewhat chastened to remember how he had struggled against Medraut's hand over his eyes, when here he was covering them anyway.

"What did he *do*?" Telemakos asked. "What did he do that your master had to cut off his hands as punishment?"

"He didn't *do* anything," the boy said, his voice savage. "He heard something. Now no one else will hear it."

"How did he hear it? Why was he there?"

"We all heard it, whatever it was," the boy said. "Anako was speaking Greek, was he not, as he always does when he doesn't want us to know what he's talking about, only afterward his secretary happened to remember that Butala understands Greek. So Butala had his tongue cut out."

"But why his hands?"

"You called your father ras, are you a prince, then? Is royalty all so stupid? So that he can't write, or gesture."

"Well, your master won't get much use of him with no hands, will he?" Telemakos said darkly.

The cat boy stared at him witheringly. "Butala wasn't ever used for his hands." He let that fall between them like lead through water. Then he added, "He's just a porter."

"Why did they have to whip him?"

"He keeps dropping things. He can't adjust his straps. The best part of the story is that he probably didn't hear anything anyway, because none of us were paying any attention to the master and his secretary, we were all too busy watching the salt merchant's little monkeys fighting one another. Who knows, who cares what the master said?"

Plague will raise the price of salt.

The dizzy rush of blood to his head made Telemakos feel as though his face was on fire. The rest of him went cold.

The cat boy said, "For God's sake, go pester someone else with your horrible questions, you ghoulish little mongrel."

There was another long, wordless shriek from the maimed porter, and Telemakos and the boy with the moustache both buried their faces again. Telemakos pressed his flaming cheeks against the fur of the beautiful mutilated cat.

Plague will raise the price of salt.

He could not find the strength to lift his head. He sat trembling in the dust at the other boy's feet, wishing desperately that he was alone in the highland savanna with his father and a herd of bushbuck, instead of waiting among these wretched people while Medraut tortured a hapless servant who was less guilty than Telemakos himself.

"Go on, go away," snapped the cat boy. "This isn't a circus."

Telemakos gathered himself and stood up. He took a deep breath.

"All right," he said. "I'm sorry about your friend."

"He's just a porter," the boy repeated bitterly, and looked away.

Alone at last again with Medraut, much later, Telemakos walked in silence. Of course, Medraut never said anything anyway, but Telemakos often spoke to him, and sometimes for him, as he had done that morning. Now he could not bring himself to speak a single word, appalled to possess knowledge worth as much as his tongue, or his hands. After a time Telemakos remembered, with renewed horror: I told the bala heg I'd been listening with Anako's porters. One of them might have said something about it to Anako. It might be my fault they noticed that boy. It might be my fault they—

He shot badly. He hit a gazelle in the rump, and it took him five more arrows to kill it. He could feel Medraut wince with each failed attempt; it always bewildered Medraut that his son could be so inaccurate an archer. After the fifth botched shot, Medraut pulled back the arrow that was notched to his own bowstring. Telemakos spoke then for the first time since they had left the roadside well, snarling at his father, "I don't need your help!"

It was late evening when they arrived at Grandfather's

country estate, and Telemakos noticed that Medraut gave him much closer attention than he usually did: helped Telemakos with his bath, saw him to his room there, brought him supper of injera bread and wat made from the meat of the gazelle they had caught on their way. Medraut sat with Telemakos while he ate, sharing his food. Then before Medraut left Telemakos alone for the night, he took the boy's head between his hands, and smoothed his son's thick white hair back gently from his forehead. He peered into Telemakos's face, his expression worried and sorrowful. Telemakos lowered his eyes respectfully to avoid meeting his father's unreadable dark blue gaze, and Medraut took his hands away and nodded a wordless good night.

Telemakos was seized with a sudden piercing hatred of his lost uncle, Lleu the Bright One, who could not know or care whether Medraut ever spoke his name again, who could never need Medraut's silence as much as Telemakos needed to hear his father's voice.

DOVES FOR THE POOR

"Light me a fire to purify this house."
22:519

TELEMAKOS THOUGHT ABOUT the challenge Goewin had set before him, the emperor's challenge. He thought about the spearmen who always stood at the door to the emperor's council chamber. He thought about Anako's maimed porter. Three months passed. So long as he kept silent, Telemakos was safe.

His mother came to interrupt him in the middle of his Greek reading, a lesson that he turned up for sporadically.

"You have a visitor," Turunesh said. "Come and attend at once."

"Who is it? What do you mean?" Telemakos dropped his reading on the floor as he jumped to his feet. He hurried to take his mother's outstretched hand, leaving his long-suffering tutor sighing elaborately as he picked up the discarded scrolls.

"The emperor invites you to a game of santaraj."

Telemakos laughed. "Who is it really?"

"The emperor wants to play chess with you," his mother repeated. "He is waiting for you in your grandfather's study."

She was serious. Telemakos felt panic rising in his throat and swallowed it, holding tightly to his mother's hand as she led him through the house.

"Really play santaraj?" he asked desperately.

"That is what he said," Turunesh answered. "So we have laid out Grandfather's best board and the ivory men from Cathay, and I shall come and serve him coffee when you have finished. Ferem will wait on you."

It was beyond protesting. Telemakos could think of no argument. He felt as though he were being led to execution.

Old Ferem waited outside Kidane's private office. He nodded to Telemakos and held open the door.

Telemakos stepped into the room and then lay flat on the floor, his face in his arms.

"Lij Telemakos," Gebre Meskal said, acknowledging him. "Please get up. Sit with me."

Telemakos obeyed silently. He had no idea what to say.

"I have not seen you in my court of late," said Gebre Meskal lightly, "or in my council."

The emperor was even younger than Goewin, barely ten years older than Telemakos. Telemakos could remember him as a beardless youth in the days before his coronation, but even then Gebre Meskal had seemed grave and ancient, his ways mysterious, his thoughts unguessable. His clothes were simple, a white kilt and shamma as plain as those Telemakos wore himself; except the emperor's shamma was clasped with a great cross embedded with emerald, and his head cloth was woven of gold-shot linen and bound with ribbons of gold mesh.

"Mother has kept me hard at work of late," Telemakos said; then he felt ashamed not to take responsibility for his own inaction. He added falteringly, "I've been neglecting my lessons. I don't excel at anything; my father deplores my shooting, my mother deplores my Greek."

"Do not demean yourself. Your aunt and my cartographer both speak highly of your skill with maps. Perhaps you will make a ship's pilot, or a navigator. Has your father taught you to reckon a path by starlight, when you hunt together?"

"Yes, Your Majesty," Telemakos stammered, stunned to receive such a compliment from the emperor.

"A good tracker reads the sky as well as the land, and understands the cries of many separate creatures," Gebre Meskal continued, looking at Telemakos thoughtfully. "You must begin to learn our several tongues. Noba is an excellent language. It comes more easily than Greek to anyone who already has Ethiopic, and the Noba chants are most musical. I shall find you a Noba tutor."

"Yes. All right," said Telemakos in surprise. "Thank you, Your Majesty."

"Come, share a game with me," said the emperor. "Your grandfather tells me you are a fair player."

I do not believe I am doing this, Telemakos thought.

He rapidly lost half a dozen contests. He did not expect to win, of course, and would not have known what to do with himself if he had won: what are you supposed to do when the emperor invites you to play a game with him, anyway? Pretend you are an idiot, or do your best to show off your intelligence? Telemakos was a mediocre player at best, he knew. He could trounce his father, but that was because Medraut had never mastered the Aksumite opening, when you and your opponent both moved your men at the same time until a piece was taken.

Telemakos was fast, fast; his strategy was to rush everybody to the front, to push as many players as possible across the board as quickly as possible. Gebre Meskal was slow, slow. He waited, waited, waited while his young opponent created elaborately complex scenarios, then brought Telemakos's intrigues crashing down with one or two patient moves. Oh, why am I doing this, Telemakos wondered, watching the emperor solemnly set the pieces up again. Gebre Meskal's narrow face was impassive; he showed no sign of either disapproval or triumph.

"Lij Telemakos," he said this time, before they began yet another ridiculous trial, "are you able to play the exact game you played last time?"

"Do you mean, repeat myself? Move the pieces in the same way?"

"Yes."

Telemakos hesitated. "I think so."

"Do it."

So he did, more slowly this time because he knew it was a lost cause.

"Attend," said Gebre Meskal, and wove one ivory pawn across the board among Telemakos's men, and took his sovereign.

They both sat silent, bent over the board. Again Telemakos found himself unable to speak.

"What did you see?" the emperor asked.

Not *What did you learn*, but *What did you see?*

"I left my king unguarded."

"Well, that's so. But that is not what I want you to see. Let's play this game again."

"This one game?" It was torment.

"Aye."

So they did, again. And again Gebre Meskal asked Telemakos, when it was swiftly ended, "What did you see?"

"Your pawn," Telemakos said slowly. "Your only pawn."

"Many would say he is the lowliest player on the board," said Gebre Meskal. "Smaller than any other. Yet he has brought down an army."

"Alone," said Telemakos. Gebre Meskal handed him back his king. Telemakos turned the piece over, then sat on his hands to keep them from trembling. "It's just a game," he said.

"It can be done," the emperor said mildly. "Tell your servant I am ready for my coffee."

Ferem went for Turunesh, and they returned together with all the equipment for a coffee ceremony. Turunesh would not let Telemakos have any, as usual, so he had to remain sitting on his hands, looking at the floor, while the emperor spoke to his mother.

"How have you found the quarantine, Woyzaro Turunesh? Does it affect the noblewomen in the heart of the capital?"

"Not especially," Turunesh answered. Telemakos noticed that her mild, unhurried manner was similar to Gebre Meskal's; why then should it be so easy to talk to her, and so impossible to talk to him?

"My father thought to sell his ships, since they may no longer trade on the Red Sea," Turunesh said. "But we should not see payment until the quarantine is lifted anyway, so we are putting two of the boats in dry dock, and the rest will have to remain at the mercy of their crews. We sent out messages to them, but of course we will not hear back. Possibly our men will find harbor across the sea in Himyar, in your cousin Abreha's kingdom."

Her hands moved automatically through the ritual of making coffee, lighting her burner, sorting the seeds for roasting.

"I worry for those men in my father's employ," Turunesh finished. "But so do I worry for us all, for Aksum. I doubt that I shall suffer any serious hardship myself."

"I'm glad," said Gebre Meskal. "It warms me to know my councilor Blatte Kidane and his daughter are with me. Perhaps you have already heard the news from Deire, where the ban on foreign trade has been taken lightly."

Deire was Aksum's most important port after Adulis,

White Deire in the far south, beyond the Salt Desert. It was the hub for Aksum's exported salt.

"What news?" Turunesh asked politely.

"Contaminated goods were allowed in, weeks ago. Pestilence has consumed Deire." He paused. "Plague has reached Aksum."

Turunesh set her earthen pot to boil. Then she hid her eyes behind one hand. She said quietly, "I wish this were not true."

"So do I," said Gebre Meskal, in tones no less calm or matter-of-fact than anything else he had said. "It is an evil truth. But the quarantine holds. Let me tell you of the ruin of Deire."

The servant began to tiptoe out. Gebre Meskal said sharply, "Please stay. It is no secret. I should like to hear this news shouted among the hornbills from treetop to treetop."

The emperor paused. There was no sound but the whisper of flames in the coffee burner.

"Deire is consuming herself," said Gebre Meskal. "She lies besieged from within, like a burning building that no one can escape, and which no one will enter.

"You know I do not want to damage my alliance with Abreha in Himyar. My admiral makes a monthly trip to the Turtle or the Hanish Islands, where he moors alongside Himyar's flagship and exchanges news with the Himyarites. But we have been cautious not to come near each other in the meetings, and no ship may return to Aksum unless under my naval escort. Other ships may leave Aksum, at any time, with appropriate authorization. They may leave, but they may not return.

"Someone has been counterfeiting my authorization, and ships have been allowed to return to Deire. Plague has come with them."

Telemakos held quiet, listening. He sat straight and polite at first, his eyes on the floor, not even daring to watch his mother make the coffee; but then as he became absorbed in Gebre Meskal's story he began to watch the butler, Ferem, who had squatted on his heels by the doorway when the emperor commanded him to stay. The old man became more and more bent as the tale went on, until he leaned with his elbows against his knees and his face hidden in his hands. He rocked back and forth on his heels, making a low, keening noise, as though in mourning.

"So we have sent a squadron of the armada to close the port, and soldiers to set a cordon around the city. Deire is guarded by a ring of fire and steel ten miles across. No one shall escape."

"They will all die, then," Turunesh said simply. She filled a cup of steaming coffee and set it before the emperor, and Telemakos marveled at the steadiness of her hands.

"We do not want to starve them. We do not want to murder them. They may no longer fish; their port is closed. We deliver tef to their boundaries, milled and ground for baking injera, and we leave it for them. We leave them beer and honey wine, goats and hens, herbs for medication. But they must build their own pyres and dig their own graves.

"No one may leave Deire. A few try; and they are struck down from a distance by the trained spears of my soldiers, and the bodies are set alight with flaming arrows. Nothing shall leave Deire. Deire is lost, that Aksum may be saved.

"Do you excuse me, lady," the emperor finished, and suddenly sank his head in his hands, like the butler. Telemakos glanced upward for a moment and saw the emperor's face wet with tears.

"Deire is lost," Gebre Meskal repeated. "It is as though I have cut off my hand to save my body from infection. I weep for Deire, White Deire of the south."

Telemakos thought of Anako, Deire's heartless and greedy archon. It seemed perfect justice that he should perish in pestilence. But what of all his company, the hapless porter Butala, the haughty young animal keeper and his black caracal, the rest of them? Plague would not pick and choose the good from the bad; there was no justice in plague, neither good nor evil. Plague was inhuman.

Gebre Meskal turned to the weeping Ferem. "Go, you may go." The old man crept out quietly. Gebre Meskal continued to speak to Telemakos's mother:

"If Deire is destroyed, I fear for Adulis, my second city, the glittering port of black basalt. Who subverted my rule in the south will sensibly move north. Perhaps the sacrifice of Deire may instruct the traitors; but I, too, have learned from this. I shall watch Adulis with care and with secrecy, from without and from within."

Then the emperor asked Turunesh a strange question.

"Tell me, Woyzaro Turunesh, would you be afraid to visit your uncle Abbas, the archon in Adulis, knowing there might be risk of plague there through practice of a black market in white salt?"

"Your Majesty—" Turunesh hesitated. "Majesty, I don't think it would worry me. If Adulis fell to plague, Aksum herself would not be far behind. There would be no escaping it. We have all the Great Valley and the Salt Desert between us and Deire, but Adulis is our sister city."

"I think so too. I'm glad you are so fearless," said the emperor. "Perhaps one day soon Lij Telemakos will want to see Adulis."

"What if . . . " Telemakos asked his mother, "what if someone asked you to do something, something important and exciting, and you did not want to do it?"

"What are you up to?" she asked.

"Not a thing."

"Ah, not a thing." Turunesh sighed. "Good. I'm glad. Help me with this one." They were caging white doves in a big basket, three dozen of their own pet doves, as alms to the Cathedral of St. Mary of Zion. This was the first time the quarantine had affected Telemakos personally: he had to sacrifice his doves so that Aksum's less fortunate might make sin offerings of them. Telemakos was sorry to see them go. But he was much better at catching the doves than his mother, so he had to help pack them. It felt like a cruel betrayal, coaxing his pets from their niche homes in the sunlit wall of the courtyard, stroking their downy breasts to gentle them still, then letting his mother truss their wings so they could not escape as she laid them in the hamper, ready for some devout sinner to wring their necks and drain their blood.

"Why must we give these away?" Telemakos asked. "Why not buy some more at market and make a donation of them?"

"They don't earn their keep. I can't justify feeding grain to fat and lazy birds, when Gedar in the villa across the way is having to sell his horses to buy tef flour. If the quarantine goes on a year or two, he will end by selling his house."

"Will we have to sell our horses? Or our house?"

"I doubt it. We don't depend on olive oil from Himyar to pay for our food, like Gedar. We can move to the estate in Adwa, and grow our own tef, if need be."

"Then why do the doves have to go, if we can afford to keep them?" Telemakos persisted.

"Because," his mother said firmly. "Because it isn't fair."

All the while they were speaking, Telemakos held a betrayed dove securely between his hands, while his mother bound fast its wings.

"Get rid of the parrots. I don't like the parrots, they bite. I like the doves."

"No one sacrifices parrots," Turunesh said. "We'll let them go."

Telemakos thought it wholly unjust that the doves, which

were sweet-natured and soft-voiced, were to be bound and slain, and their bodies burned; while the parrots, which were bad-tempered and noisy, got set free.

His mother had not forgotten his original question. "Tell me about this 'not a thing' that you don't want to do," she said. "Is it a dare from another boy? Have you found a playmate at last?"

Telemakos made a point of keeping quiet about the difficulties he had with other children. "I don't play," he said scornfully.

"O silent tracker of lions," his mother teased, "I did not mean to insult you. I worry that you are lonely."

Telemakos laughed in surprise. "I am never lonely." He bent over another caught dove, whistling and cooing.

"You have no best companion."

"So I have. Goewin is my best companion."

His mother laughed in turn. "Telemakos, that is not what I mean. As you know. But what's your challenge, sweet heart, that you don't like? And who's challenged you?"

Telemakos answered seriously, "I can't tell you who. I'm no tale-teller; and I can't tell you what it is, either." He went back to the niches in the wall to trap another dove. He was beginning to be sorry he had said anything.

"If you will hide the heart of the matter, sweet one, I can't give you the best advice. But let me ask you this: Why don't you want to do this thing? Is it a game? Is it silly? Is it pointless?"

"I said it was important, and it is."

"Will it harm anyone? Help anyone? Will good or evil come of it? Do not answer, ask yourself. Is it something you shouldn't do, or something you don't want to do?"

"I think it is something I should do," Telemakos said slowly. "But I don't want to."

"Why not, then?" Turunesh took the fluttering dove from his hands.

Telemakos waited until she had finished with the bird, then pressed himself close against her to make his mother hold him. He stood clasped in her arms, looking down at the imprisoned doves, and whispered, "I am afraid to do it."

Turunesh spoke calmly, her voice normal and matter-of-fact as she stroked his hair. "Can't someone else do it, then?"

"I don't think so," Telemakos answered, and tried to speak as calmly as Turunesh. "Not so well as I could, anyway."

She laughed at him, and held him close. "What if you weren't afraid?"

"I'd do it."

She let go of him, and set the lid on the basket. "Thank you for helping me, Telemakos. I know it makes you sad to lose these friends."

"It's all right. I'd rather do it myself than hide and sulk and make someone else do a nasty job in my place."

Telemakos suddenly felt the strength in his knees turn to water. He had to kneel and lay his head on the lid of the basket, stricken. "Oh."

His mother knelt beside him, one hand on his shoulder

and the other on his hair again. "Sweet heart, my little one, I'm so sorry."

He let her think he was mourning for the doves. But that was not what had struck him down. It was hearing himself speak aloud what he would have to do.

In the Lion's Den

" . . . in the palace now.
My mother knows nothing of this. No servants either."
2:452–53

LEARNING THE SCHEDULE of the emperor's council was easy. Telemakos had only to lean casually outside the door to Grandfather's study on a few occasions, and to lie among the oil jars in the antechamber to Grandfather's reception hall.

Getting into the council room in the New Palace was not so simple. The door was always guarded, but once Telemakos knew when the bala heg convened, before and after their meetings he was able to slip in with the butlers. He could even manage this without having to hide, by scavenging broken buns from the trays that were set out for the council's refreshment; the guards and butlers tolerated him begging at their heels because he was familiar, and because they knew he was vaguely royal. It was tempting to take advantage of this ease of access, but Telemakos did not dare seem particularly interested in any one room.

He spent an entire day pestering a couple of cleaners, following them all over the New Palace, and so made his most valuable discovery regarding the council room: it had a latrine with a slotted window backing over one of the training yards. Telemakos stood on the waste box, surreptitiously, and easily slipped his head and shoulders through the window. It would have been too narrow for a grown man. Telemakos pulled his head back inside and looked up. The walls were close enough to climb if you leaned your back against one and braced your legs against the other; the ceiling was low. There was a ledge high along the wall behind the waste box, and when Telemakos reached up to explore it, he felt a little wind play about his hands. The ledge led to a chimney that was somehow connected to the closet above.

Telemakos jumped lightly to the floor. No one was paying any attention to him. He took hold of the curtain that separated the council room from its antechamber and flapped it back and forth exuberantly.

"You want to give this a good dusting," he said to the cleaners.

He discovered that the privy window was guarded from without only when the council was in session, presumably to stop anyone listening beneath it. The window was set in the outside wall at thrice Telemakos's height. There was a ledge at the level of the room's floor that ran beneath the window, beneath the screened window of the council room itself, and at last, beneath another window twenty feet farther along.

It can't be so simple, Telemakos thought. Surely they guard that entrance. Why, an *assassin* could climb up there and hide in the chimney—

Not unless he were a dwarf. They're well guarded against other men, against one another. But they have no fear of children.

Telemakos needed to be sure he could do it, and he thought he needed at least two days in the New Palace to put the entire plan into practice. When next his father appeared and seemed to show interest in taking him hunting, Telemakos told him that he could not escape his new instruction in Noba. He did plan to attend these lessons, partly because he did not like to lie to his father, and partly because it would give Telemakos a reason to be at large in the New Palace. He told his mother that he was hunting with Medraut, an untruth so easy it felt unfair. Medraut would never tell Turunesh otherwise, and she would never ask him; and Karkara, the Noba tutor, would surely not complain to anyone that Telemakos had in fact turned up for a lesson.

Telemakos needed days alone. He did not want the pressure of having to sneak or wheedle his way out of the palace after the gates were closed for the night, and he needed darkness to test and enact his plan.

In darkness Telemakos made his way through the dim furnishings of the deserted audience chamber next to the council room. He wound his shamma around his waist, tying it out of his way, and crawled out the window. In darkness he edged himself across the ledge above the training yard, until he gained the narrow air vent to the council's latrine; he crawled through the opening and into deeper darkness.

This much had gone reassuringly well. The true test, now, was to see if the chimney could be used as a hiding place. His success hung on this, Telemakos felt; if not, he would have to be content with wrapping himself in the folds of the privy curtain and hoping no one pulled it away, or climbing to the ceiling if anyone came in and hoping no one looked up.

He walked up the walls, his back to one and his feet to the other in the blind dark, until he was level with the ledge. The gap above the ledge was less high than the length of a man's foot. Telemakos put his head through, and choked and pulled it out again. The stench was overwhelming. He held himself rigid between the walls for a few seconds, gasping, then climbed down and took off his clothes. He climbed back up and put his head and shoulders and one arm through the gap. He breathed lightly through his mouth this time, and could almost taste the smell, but his hand told him the walls were clean and dry. The boxes were emptied daily, he knew; only the smell remained.

Somehow he managed to twist and tease his body up into the airshaft, until he was standing on the ledge. The darkness was utter in here: it made no difference whether he opened or closed his eyes. The space was barely wider than his body. He could not stand free of both walls at once. It was like being entombed.

Mother of God, how did I get my legs in? How do I get out again?

Getting out the first time was a struggle. He managed it at last only driven by panic; his ribs and knees and elbows caught every flaw in the stone walls and every corner of the waste box as he tumbled to the floor.

"Oh!"

He lay in a breathless heap, coughing and barking with the effort not to yell. Then he began to choke with hysterical laughter at the thought of how he would explain himself if he ended up trapped in the airshaft of the bala heg's latrine.

The worst part of the whole exercise was making himself climb into the airshaft for the second time. He practiced getting in and out until it became, while not exactly easy, at least fast and fluid. He knew what he was doing now, and could do it quickly and quietly.

By the time he made his way back through the palace corridors they were still and empty. There was no light in the Golden Court. The fountains were off for the night. Telemakos washed quietly in one of the pools, rather desperate to be rid of the smell of the airshaft. He lay full length in the dark water and held his breath while he rinsed his hair, then got out and sat shivering on the fountain's rim. Here it was that Goewin had set him this challenge. With light fingers Telemakos touched the wide lip of the pool, the stone surface that Goewin had used as her desk. When he was dry, he wrapped his shamma tightly around his shoulders, settled himself in his favorite hiding place among the Golden Court's reeds and palms, and went to sleep.

He dreamed he was stuck in the airshaft. The opening at the bottom was sealed shut, and he could not breathe. He woke up struggling and gasping and trying to cry out, tangled in his shamma. Esato was crouching next to him with her hands clamped over his nose and mouth; Sofya knelt opposite her. Telemakos tore Esato's hands away.

"You pair of vultures!" he hissed. "What do you think you're doing?"

"What do you think *you're* doing, sneaking little crossbreed?" Sofya whispered back. "This isn't a wayside inn!"

"He, he, he," Esato giggled. "He's got pond weed in his hair."

Telemakos sat up and ran a hand over his head. It was daylight, but only just. The fountains were not on yet.

"Do they always set you loose this early?" he asked, and crawled out of the palm bed. The twins followed him, both of them giggling now.

"We're to have breakfast with Our Mother. Every third week," Sofya said. "Come with us, if you're not hiding from anyone in particular this time."

He considered this. Candake, queen of queens, the emperor's aunt, was fond of Telemakos. It would be a good way to spend the day, and he could count on being fed, as well.

"You do look a state," Sofya said critically. "Has your grandfather made you leave home? What are you doing here, in truth?"

"I stayed past curfew. I didn't want to argue with the guards to let me out, so I came in here." And this was true enough, though Telemakos knew the Golden Court was lost to him now; he had been found out beneath the palms by no less than three different people in the past three months, and he could not count on hiding here again.

"You've been fighting, too."

His elbows and knees were scraped raw.

"Look, it's none of your business," Telemakos said shortly.

"It is if we take you to breakfast," Sofya said mildly. "Come on. Our Mother will want to fix your hair."

Candake did not ask him any questions. She roared with laughter when she saw Telemakos, and made him kneel between her enormous knees while she fussed over his head with combs and oil and clarified butter. She was a great admirer of his hair; in recent years this had driven Telemakos to avoid her company, although he liked her, and she let him drink coffee.

"Put his hair in a thousand plaits," suggested Sofya, and Esato giggled again.

"He's not a girl," grunted Candake. The queen of queens was the size of about six women together; she ate constantly, and laughed like an hysterical hyena. She had attendants who helped her to move. Telemakos was fairly certain that seldom as he saw her she gave him more attention than she gave to her own daughters. "Eh, Telemakos Meder, tell me. How fares the princess Goewin, the terrible British ambassador? How is my little queen of Sheba? Her quarantine is bringing ruin on us."

"It's the emperor's quarantine," Telemakos dared to object in Goewin's defense.

"It was her idea."

"Does everyone blame it on her?" Telemakos asked, curious.

"Many do," Candake wheezed, and chose another comb.

"That's most unjust," Telemakos said. "Goewin only advised it be done. No one was forced to act on her advice. And see what happened in Deire."

"He knows so much about it," commented Sofya, sitting despondently at her mother's feet with her face between her hands, her body arranged in a very tableau of boredom. "I thought we were to have breakfast this morning, Our Mother. Esato's hungry."

"I'm hungry," echoed Esato.

"She would have eaten the boy if I had not rescued him."

Esato grinned at Telemakos, and Candake gave one of her deep-throated chuckles. "Yes, yes, my silly babies. But indulge me this silver hair a moment longer, and this boy's talk. The Tame Lion, my imperial nephew, is too busy for coffee with his old auntie, too serious to talk while he eats, and I am too fat and slow to chase him into his study when he has his Hour Alone. Telemakos Meder will tell me all the courtly news."

Telemakos was suddenly alert.

"The Tame Lion, you mean the emperor. What's his 'Hour Alone'? Does he have a private study?"

Sofya said darkly, "Don't tell him anything, Our Mother. He's a little spy."

But it was Sofya herself who pointed out the emperor's private study to Telemakos when he excused himself for his Noba lesson in the afternoon, and who told him how often the emperor came and went from it, and who guarded it.

"Who's the spy?" Telemakos said. "How do you know all this?"

"Gebre Meskal is my cousin," Sofya said loftily. "Oh, go away, Esato, let go of me." She slapped her sister's hands from her skirts. "Yes, I know you're scared of Karkara, but no one else is. Get *off*!"

The actual afternoon in the council room the following day was anticlimactic for Telemakos after the trial run. He installed himself in the antechamber after dark the night before, and slept wrapped in the curtain; he hid in the airshaft while the caterers prepared the room, and sat comfortably on the privy floor while the bala heg was in session. Telemakos heard everything; indeed, he could see more from beneath the curtain than he had been able to see in full view of the councilors, with his face to the wall.

He had one bad moment when someone came into the privy. He saw the man rising from his seat on the council—it was the young one, Ityopis, the twins' elder brother. Telemakos fled up the chimney without trouble, but standing there he suddenly realized he had no way to hide his feet. The airway was too narrow for him to bend his knees or to turn himself sideways. He finally held himself up by bracing his hands against the end walls. He managed to hang there until he heard Ityopis leave, and he thought that was the absolute limit of his strength; he nearly wept when someone else came in before he even had a chance to shake the numbness from his hands or get his breath back. But no one noticed him.

When it was over, he had to hide in the airshaft again while the cleaners did their work; but he could not escape the room until it was dark. He sat on the floor to wait for nightfall, his mind full of the meeting. It had been particularly dull, much talk of taxes and revenues, which Telemakos found tedious and difficult to remember. He repeated patiently to himself all that he had learned.

He had been in this one room for nearly a day now with nothing to eat or drink, and long before dark he was so thirsty that everything else began to go out of his head.

Why had he not considered this in his plan? He would die rather than give himself up now, just because he had nothing to drink. He waited stubbornly, licking dry lips, his head beginning to ache. Even after night fell he forced himself to wait another hour to give the palace time to grow quiet. Then he climbed back through the narrow window and across the ledge on the outside wall, and discovered courtiers drinking and laughing in the room he meant to escape through.

You lot of bushpig herders, he cursed them silently.

He listened at the window for a few minutes. The men were boasting to one another about their horses. It was interesting, but not worth listening to while clinging to the wall in the dark and going mad with thirst.

Telemakos spidered back to the council room and climbed back in, and wandered about checking the baskets and bureaus in case anyone had left any refreshments behind. But the cleaners had been thorough, and there was nothing. The outer door was barred and guarded, Telemakos knew; he could not get out that way. He waited another two hours, judging by the moon, and tried the neighboring room again. The party was still going on.

Well, I can't stand this, Telemakos thought, and lowered himself as far as he could off the ledge, and dropped into the training yard below.

The fall knocked all the breath from him, for the second time in as many days. For a few minutes he lay flat on his face vowing not to do this to himself again anytime soon. Then he began to think about what to do next. He was not sure he would be able to get back inside the main building at this time of night, and even if he did, where would he go? He wanted a drink more than anything in the world. His mouth felt as though he had swallowed a jugful of sand, and his head was pounding. He would not be welcome in the kitchens; he smelled like a sewer, and he could not bathe in the Golden Court again, where the royal crocodiles Esato and Sofya would be watching for him. He could go home as soon as the gates were opened in the morning, but he had to find something to drink *now*—

There was always fresh water in the lion pit. There was never any guard.

Sheba was out on her nightly rounds, prowling the palace grounds, but Solomon was snoring gently beneath the pencil cedars.

"Lazy old beast," Telemakos whispered.

Solomon recognized his friend in spite of the stink. He shared his water willingly. He would never tell a soul Telemakos had been there. Telemakos buried his face in Solomon's mane and felt loved.

He stayed in the lion pit all that night; but even he did not dare to sleep there.

His mother scowled with concern the next morning when Telemakos presented himself on Grandfather's front steps, and wrinkled her nose in disgust. Telemakos bowed his head and waited for her exclamation of disapproval.

"You're taking care of your hair, I see," she commented.

He laughed, and saw her smiling.

"Go take a bath," she said, which was what she usually said when he came back from a hunting trip.

He was clean, fed and rested, and wound up like a spring when he ran back to the New Palace in the afternoon. He actually made it to his Noba lesson for the third time in that week. It helped to calm him, sitting in the sunlight of Karkara's office and watching the weary-looking official build towers with the small tablets of salt that were piled on his table, while he told Telemakos stories in the language of his childhood and listened absently as Telemakos repeated them. Both their minds ran elsewhere, Karkara's to the pile of documents in the basket at his feet, and Telemakos's to his next great challenge: making his way unseen into the emperor's study for the Hour Alone.

Telemakos made use of his friends the butlers once again. He had to endure a few nerve-racking moments while one of them forgot to remove a tray and came back for it. He had another fright when two young soldiers sifted through the wall hangings with their spears a few minutes before Gebre Meskal arrived; once, long ago, Telemakos had narrowly missed being run through in just such a search. But when the emperor at last came into his private study, Telemakos was sitting coolly beneath the window, legs crossed and hands folded in his lap.

He hesitated a fraction of a second before he bowed, to let the emperor see him there. Then he fell on his face on the leopard skin at Gebre Meskal's feet.

"Well played, Lij Telemakos," said the emperor.

Telemakos smiled, his face hidden in his hands, elated.

"Get up and sit with me. Are you hungry?"

"I'm all right, thank you, Your Majesty."

"Sit here. Tell me what you know. I take it you mean to tell me of the council yesterday? Please begin."

Telemakos dutifully repeated as much as he could remember of the meeting. Gebre Meskal listened with the same air of detached interest that he had shown in Telemakos's santaraj playing. When Telemakos finished, Gebre Meskal said, "This is all true, and well spoken, but there is nothing here you could not have learned from your grandfather, if he were minded to tell you. There were no secrets passed in yesterday's meeting. And I cannot trust you as my emissary unless you can bring me proof that you were there: an object, a token, perhaps."

"I am not a thief," said Telemakos coldly.

"I need proof."

"You stayed behind after the others left," Telemakos said. "You looked inside the mesob basket table, and underneath the podium, and behind the privy curtain, trying to find me out. And when you found no one, you sighed, and spoke aloud, saying, 'Perhaps it is wrong to expect so much of a child.' "

There was a long, long silence. Gebre Meskal rubbed at his beard, and Telemakos thought he was trying to hide a smile that kept creeping across his solemn face. "Where were you?" the emperor asked.

"Should I tell?"

"Well, your proof is sufficient. But now tell me something I don't already know."

Telemakos looked down at his hands, turning them back and forth in his lap. Then he laid them on the mesob table between them. "I don't suppose you know this," Telemakos began slowly.

"Anako, the Deire archon who was in Aksum at the beginning of the season, had a conversation with a salt merchant while he was here," Telemakos said. "They were talking of a black market in salt to open in Arsinoë, and they meant the conversation to be secret. Or private, anyway. One of Anako's porters overheard them, and was punished for it. I heard them, too, but they didn't know I was listening, so I wasn't punished. The porter had his tongue cut out. And they cut his hands off."

Telemakos rapped his hands against the table.

"So maybe you were right," he finished. "Maybe what you want is too much to expect from me."

"You could do it."

"I know I could."

Gebre Meskal stood up and crossed the room. From one of the carven shelves that hung by the wall he took a miniature santaraj set.

"Show me your game again," said Gebre Meskal. "That game we played three times in your mother's house."

It took some concentration for Telemakos to re-create the fiasco, but he did at last successfully.

"Now here comes my small pawn," said Gebre Meskal. "Here he comes, moving among the enemies all on his own. Do you see? He acts alone, but he is not alone. He has an army behind him, also, my army; and with our lives we will fight to defend him."

Telemakos clenched his fists, and opened them again, and closed them again. He did not have to do this. He looked out the window; he looked at the leopard-skin rug. He looked at his hands, and opened them carefully. He remembered that Butala's punishment might well have been his fault. In some sense, then, this task was already his responsibility.

He asked slowly, "What do you want me to do?"

"I want you to go to Adulis," said the emperor, "and discover who would sabotage my quarantine."

GOEWIN AND HER BROTHERS

" . . . he slipped into the enemy's city, roamed its streets—"
4:276

"DON'T TELL RAS MEDER," Telemakos insisted. "He won't let me do it."

The arrangements were in place for his visit to Adulis. His mother would go with him, ostensibly to visit her uncle; Kidane's brother Abbas was the archon there, the governor of Adulis. Turunesh could see to Kidane's dry-docked ships. It made sense for her to go, and to take her son, who had never seen his own land farther than Kolöe. Goewin would go as well. Her reason for being in Adulis was more obscure, to do with seeking out final messages from her homeland among the warehoused shipping. Her real reason was that she was Gebre Meskal's conspirator, and it was to her that Telemakos must answer and make his reports.

But Goewin refused to leave Aksum until she had told

Medraut of their plan. She and Telemakos hiked above the city to the monastery Abba Pantelewon, hoping to find Medraut there.

"You did not even tell the bala heg about me," Telemakos argued.

"We did not tell the bala heg for your own protection," said Goewin. "The fewer folk who know about you, the better. But we told your grandfather and your mother, and we will tell your father."

"He will refuse his permission, I know it. He will want to do the work himself."

"Well, he might, Telemakos," said Goewin. "If anyone is your equal at underhanded stalking, it is your father. He tracked me from Britain to Aksum without my knowing it, four thousand miles, to see to my safety. I doubt not he would do the same for you. But I can't see him doing it for Gebre Meskal, because Gebre Meskal wants to hear a report; and as you know, Medraut never tells anybody anything."

"Why, Goewin?" Telemakos asked.

"Why what?"

They climbed along the wooded hillside above the city, Telemakos walking ahead of Goewin up the narrow path, because she could see over his head.

"Why won't he speak?"

Goewin did not answer immediately. Telemakos glanced back at her and saw that she had taken an arrow from her quiver and was using it to swat leaves and twigs away from her face. She never went anywhere without her bow. She walked in the city streets without a guard, as well.

She answered gently, "Telemakos, my love, I told you what I think about it. He is punishing himself because he could not save my twin brother. You have more of him than anyone else, even your mother. No one can have all of him."

Telemakos swiped at the leaves himself. He said softly, "I want him to love me as much as he loved Lleu."

Behind him, Goewin gave a bark of black hilarity. "God blind me, Telemakos, do you have any idea how much he hated Lleu?"

"I do not believe you."

"Medraut was so jealous of Lleu he meant to murder him. He poisoned Lleu. He kept him sleepless for four days, till Lleu started to see things that weren't there and thought he would go mad. When my aunt Morgause held Lleu's life for ransom, in her lust for power and vengeance over my father, Medraut joined her. He dragged Lleu hundreds of miles through frozen wilderness, meaning to deliver him to death at her hands. Oh—I cannot speak of the evil Medraut did. I came near to killing him myself."

"I do not believe you," Telemakos repeated stubbornly.

"I started to beat his head in with the end of a spear. I would have killed him, Telemakos. I wanted to avenge the wrong he'd done my brother. Only Lleu would not let me."

They walked without speaking for a few minutes. Then Goewin said in a low voice, "I'm sorry. I wish I had not told you this. I love your father, Telemakos. But I loved my twin, also. Lleu was cruel to Medraut as well; they were both at fault. But they kissed and forgave each other at the end of it, and then Lleu was killed in the battle of Camlan before the season was out. I think Medraut's silence is his penance, his own punishment on himself for not making amends to Lleu by saving his life at Camlan."

"He's not punishing himself," said Telemakos. "He's punishing me and everyone else. What good does his silence do for anyone, your Lleu especially?"

"I've often envied Medraut his ease of washing his hands of those around him," Goewin agreed. "Look, here we are. I'll wait for you."

Only men and boys were allowed in the monastery.

Telemakos went ahead on his own. The monks at the gate welcomed him; they knew him, and knew whom he was looking for. Telemakos waited in the courtyard and tried to imagine a younger version of his father, eaten with envy enough to poison the small brother whom he also loved. But no, not small: Lleu would then have been a young man, Goewin's twin brother, dark haired and white faced and imperious. Telemakos tried to picture him, but his mind would only offer up a dark-haired image of himself.

He thought of Medraut twisting his arm behind him and holding him blind. Medraut had done that to protect Telemakos; but how could Lleu have felt, held like that in malice, in fear for his life? How could you ever bear such betrayal?

Yet Lleu had forgiven him, said Goewin, and her implication was that she had, too; Telemakos was sure. But Medraut had not forgiven himself. Maybe he felt that no one else had, either.

Telemakos thought Adulis was hell and heaven on earth. It was too hot: he had never been out of the highlands before, and the heavy heat exhausted him. Walking through the sweltering air was like swimming through warm water. He could not run. It was too buggy: everyone sat about in the dark after the sun set, because if you left a light burning it drew the mosquitoes, and you were eaten alive. A tenth of the city was constantly stricken with ague, but no one seemed to care.

Telemakos was supposed to be at work now, an agent of the emperor, but he felt as if he were on holiday. His language lessons were abandoned, and the exercises in drawing maps, and the grueling hours of archery beneath his father's grimaces. Instead Telemakos roamed the market stalls and city plazas, and rode his pony to nearby Gabaza, where the wharves stood baking and still and the sea air smelled of buttery smoke and spice. There was a great fanfare when the armada's flagship made its monthly trip to the Turtle Islands to exchange shouted news reports with Abreha's commander. Fewer and fewer ships docked in the harbor as the season ran on, but fleets of little fishing boats still came and went with their naval escorts. Commerce was not suffering in Adulis under the quarantine. It had become the focus for Aksum's internal trade in salt since the destruction of Deire. Everywhere Telemakos went, people were buying and selling salt, using salt to pay for other things, or talking about salt.

Goewin interviewed Telemakos before he went to bed each night. When she finished, his mother would come in and kiss him, and it looked to all as though his aunt and his mother were taking turns at settling him to sleep.

"Didn't Medraut get on your nerves, following you all the way from Britain?" Telemakos asked Goewin.

"I never knew he was there."

"He follows me everywhere," said Telemakos. "I can smell him."

"Oh, Telemakos!" Goewin rocked with laughter, sitting on the edge of his cot. "I suspected it was to keep an eye on you that he came with us. What does he smell like?"

"Incense, like a priest, and the herbs and spirits he uses for medicine. And sometimes he smells of blood, when he's been hunting. But it adds up to him, do you see, Ras Meder, none other."

"And what do I smell like?" Goewin quickly put her hand over Telemakos's mouth to keep him from answering. "Stop, don't tell me, I'm jesting. That's why Gebre Meskal chose you as his scout, and not me. I can't recognize people by their smell."

The monsoon came. In the Aksumite highlands this was the winter season of the Long Rains, though in coastal Adulis it was perpetual sultry summer. The salt caravans arrived only sporadically now. The desert sun would be too searing for traffic, and the Long Rains in the highlands would make roads impassable for the next three months. Adulis was accustomed to this, and settled itself for the monsoon season.

Telemakos knew the city well by now, and with his help Goewin had drawn diagrams of all the markets and most of the permanent stalls in them. They made lists of the merchants and where they preferred to trade. Telemakos found that when people had nothing to buy or sell, they spent their time talking instead: beneath the awnings of the market stalls until the morning mist burned off over the palm and thatch, then moving indoors to the shade of the shops and beer sellers when the sticky heat became unbearable. Telemakos listened.

One morning a few weeks into the monsoon, he turned back into a little residential square he had just crossed, and called out his father's name.

"Ras Meder!"

There was no answer, of course; but when Telemakos stalked back across the square, Medraut was sitting on a stone bench under the protection of a cluster of date palm, openly waiting for him.

"Please, my lord, please listen. You can't follow me today. I'll tell you where I'm going, but you mustn't follow."

Medraut held open his hands; it meant, Why not? or, What are you telling me? or, How can I let you go alone?

"You make everyone suspicious. They see you and they shut up. You are too foreign, too strange. They wonder why you never speak, they wonder why you always carry a bow. People will notice me if they see us together, they'll see my hair and connect me to you. Please, Ras Meder. I need to be invisible."

Medraut touched Telemakos's hair and shook his head.

His stony eyes said nothing, but his expression spoke all of love and worry.

"I am safer without you, Ras Meder," said Telemakos. "I am. No one sees me. Even when they see me, they don't see me."

He heard the cocksure confidence in his own voice and thought that his father would never buy this line of argument. But he had to get rid of Medraut. He could not pass unnoticed in a gang of dock children with any credibility when there was a chance someone was going to spot his father lurking on the other side of the quay.

"Wait for me in the next street, if you like," Telemakos offered, desperate even for a compromise.

His father nodded. Telemakos knelt spontaneously and kissed his hands. "Oh, thank you, thank you, sir. I will take care, I will, you have my word."

Telemakos asked Goewin, "Has Gebre Meskal other scouts here in Adulis? Other than me, I mean."

She hesitated before she answered. "There is a system in place for all Adulis. Each answers to someone else, and the separate hierarchies are not known to anyone but the emperor himself."

She paused, and Telemakos waited expectantly, sitting up in bed with his hands clasped around his knees. Goewin sighed. She said, "I know a little more than most, because—because you are so unusual among his servants. Why do you ask?"

"Has he men who secretly patrol the dockyard in Gabaza?"

"Yes, Gebre Meskal has set sentries over the harbor here. Some are secret, some are not."

"I think I know who they are; and I think two of them are false to the emperor. Well, I know they are false, but I am not sure they are in Gebre Meskal's service."

Telemakos saw Goewin's whole body go taut. She jumped up from his bedside and paced the two steps across his little room in the governor's mansion. The window was curtained with gossamer to bar the insects, and there was a pot of mosquito smudge burning on the windowsill. Goewin stood at the window and smacked the palm of her hand lightly against the frame, scarcely able to contain her excitement.

"I knew you could do this, Telemakos, I knew you could. I have been waiting *so long* to test you in this—" She cut herself off.

"Let me be quiet. Tell me. Tell me who it is. Tell me what you've heard."

"Well: there is illegal trading. And it is mostly salt, I think, though I do hear Beja tribesmen muttering that they want to get their emeralds to Persia. Nothing is happening now, nothing ever happens when it is winter in the highlands. But when the monsoon winds change—"

Telemakos had pieced this together slowly; it had taken him some while to learn to tell real intrigue from wild rumor.

"There is a cabal of men who are waiting payment, in gold, for last season's shipment. Since the border with Sasu is blocked, they send the gold by boat now. They are mostly

Himyarite ships; you could send a message to Abreha and see if he can stop it happening at his end. The next payment is to be put ashore near Samidi, our northern port, up the coast from here."

Goewin slammed a fist against the windowsill, making the smudge pot jump. "What, have they learned nothing from Deire? A city destroyed, and still we covet gold so much! What earthly good will it do anyone when we all lie blackened and twisted in the streets?"

Telemakos waved at her to stop. "They have learned a little. Those who deliver the shipment stack it on the beach and build a pyre around it. They send the whole thing up in flames, to purify it, before they leave again. The payment must be in gold or something else that won't be destroyed by fire. The Beja think they can sell their emeralds by this cunning, as well, but I don't think they've tried it."

Goewin asked softly, "Do you know how they slip the emperor's net?"

"Someone authorizes the ships that leave. Someone important, some official. Possibly a noble, probably the same who gave the authorizations for Deire." Telemakos added quickly, "It's not the governor. Not Abbas."

"It may have been the governor of Deire, but the archon of Adulis doesn't have that power anymore," said Goewin. "Since Deire's ruin the authorization must come from Aksum, from the imperial city itself. A tedious process. But this means that someone in Aksum—"

Telemakos hugged his knees to his chest, waiting for

Goewin to speak aloud the dreadful conclusion. But when she spoke again her tone was mild, if weary. "Well. So, there is treachery all around us. Ugh, I am so naïve. I never dreamed this quarantine would prove so difficult. I thought a land as powerful and self-sufficient as Aksum should be glad to save herself.

"Do you have any idea who's behind this scheme?" she finished.

"None, my lady." Telemakos yawned behind his knees.

"We need to destroy this at its heart. We need to discover those who rule this trade." She was not talking to him; she was thinking aloud. "By God, I'll question those sentries myself."

"What do you want me to do?" Telemakos yawned again.

She knelt by his bedside and kissed him. "I want you to go to sleep."

"I will, but tell me what to do."

"Listen," Goewin said. "Only continue to listen."

A Dogfight

And now Telemachus . . .
the howling dogs went nuzzling up around him,
not a growl as he approached.
16:4–6

TELEMAKOS WANTED TO get inside the royal mint in Adulis. He was certain that this was where the smugglers met, once a fortnight, to plan their next campaign, in the place where they melted and recast their tainted gold. One of the foremen there let them in.

The guard dogs had become Telemakos's greatest challenge. He could make his way in and out, but he could not stay because of the dogs. He could negotiate the sentries, and the zareba barrier of baled desert thorn, and the stone drainage channel scarcely wider than a man's leg; that was his doorway to the mint. But the guard dogs would not leave him alone. He could sweet them, he could quiet them, he could bribe them, he was sure none of them would ever hurt him. He could not get them to leave him alone.

Telemakos realized with delight that he had found a task to set his father.

"Ras Meder," he asked, "You know how to poison someone without killing him, don't you?"

Medraut stared at him. He took hold of Telemakos's wrist, imprisoning him. What the devil do you mean by that? or, Where in God's name did you hear that? was what his look said.

"You're a doctor. You know such things."

Medraut gave a derisive snort and let go. He looked away.

"I need to make some dogs go to sleep," Telemakos persisted. "I thought you could show me how."

Medraut glanced up. After a long pause he nodded slowly.

"*Thank you,* sir."

Every time Medraut agreed to help him it was like receiving an unexpected gift.

The night of the smugglers' meeting was unexpectedly wretched. The suffocating air went suddenly cool and breezy for an hour after sunset, while lightning licked the far edge of the sky; then the monsoon began to whip the palms half over on their sides, and the rain beat down so hard it stung. Telemakos went out wearing only shirt, kilt, and sandals. He never expected to be cold in Adulis, and a shamma would get tangled in the thorns or mire him as he crawled through the culvert. Nor did he feel confident climbing and hiding when he was wearing boots. He was wet as a drowned cat, and freezing, five minutes after he left the governor's mansion.

When Telemakos had first found the spillway he used as a

passage into the mint, it was clogged with dried grass and sand, and he had wondered why anyone had bothered to build such a substantial drainage system in torrid Adulis. Now he knew. Rainwater poured in rivers through the gutter. He hated getting in anyway; he had already made several trials, and though it got easier, he never felt any better about it. The culvert was not long, but it was unforgivingly narrow. Some part of Telemakos's body—either his head or his feet—always stuck out one end or the other, making him vulnerable. He could not crawl through the channel without a feeling of deep dread that someone was going to catch hold of his feet and pull him back.

Once through in either direction it was all right. There were wonderful places to hide within the walls of the mint: vats and work baskets, open fretwork beneath trays and benches, stone cupboards and niches, spaces that seemed too small for anything bigger than a mongoose. Telemakos's chief fear tonight was that he would leave trails of water wherever he went.

The dogs gave him no trouble. With Medraut's help he was able to drug them, all but two. One of these was usually chained, and made a great deal of noise at intruders, and the other always lost interest in Telemakos after a few minutes. These two were his decoys. With the rest of them quiet, Telemakos was free to make his way through the building at will.

He was there first. The smugglers used a different room for each meeting, he knew, so he could only wait for them before he chose a spot to settle in. He prowled through the likely workshops, scouting for good hiding places. He ended in a corner where he found a banked fire. It was under a roofed porch, open to the air at the side; but it was in the lee of the wind, and Telemakos could not resist the glowing furnace.

Neither could the six men who were meeting there. They came straggling in wringing out their shammas and cursing the weather. Telemakos lay full length beneath a granite trough meant for channeling molten metal, and silently cursed with them. The fire was too far across the enclosure to make much difference to him.

He watched and listened. The men drank steaming cups of honey wine and complained loudly that the mint was losing money because of the emperor's order to debase his own gold coins. One of them seemed to be lamenting gold coinage as a lost craft; Telemakos thought this man a pompous oaf, trying to impress the others. Telemakos was beginning to shiver. He wished they would get to the point.

So did their leader, a foreman from the mint. "Stop moaning," he told them. "The new year will bring far Sasu's best gold ore, and then it won't matter to you what Gebre Meskal puts in his coins."

"If the Lazarus can put through the warrant for the shipping of the gold."

"He will. He brings the warrant himself from the Authority."

"He won't. He doesn't like to touch it. He'll ask the Authority to send it by imperial courier. Word is the Lazarus will go straight to the Afar salt mines next season, and bypass Adulis. He's scared of Adulis. The emperor has watchmen here; there are too many people who might know him."

The Authority? *The Lazarus?*

"The Lazarus isn't scared of the emperor's sleuthhounds," the pompous craftsman sneered, and spat. "He's scared of plague. He doesn't trust his own racket to keep it out. He barely missed being caught in Deire, and now he stays away from the coast."

Telemakos could not stop shivering. He tried to curl himself into a ball, but there was not enough room.

"What's that?" asked the craftsman.

The foreman answered, "Rats. They're everywhere, this close to the water. The dogs have grown fat and lazy feasting on them. So now, tell me again what you said, because I have not heard your news. Do you mean we shall not see the Lazarus at all next season?"

"I said, he's going to the Afar mines himself, to oversee the cutting. But he won't pick up his payment here. We're to send it to Aksum."

Who in blazes is 'the Lazarus'?

"And the Authority's payment?"

"All of it."

"Damned rats," said the man who had not spoken a word since the wine was poured. He scooped up a handful of the scrap tin nuggets that lay about the mouth of the furnace and began to sling them low across the yard, into corners and alcoves. He lashed one straight into Telemakos's face.

It caught the edge of his eyebrow. For a moment he thought it had hit him in the eye. He whipped his head around and sank his teeth into his forearm. The noise of wind and rain and rats covered any sound he might have made.

"It's not rats," said the cynical know-it-all with the news. "Someone's listening. Adulis is full of spies."

Lying half-blinded and freezing beneath the stone trough, Telemakos had the presence of mind to realize that they had neither seen nor heard him: they were simply nervous. The silent one stood up and strode to the edge of the covered porch, where the rain blew in. He peered into the dark factory yard.

"I think you're right," he said.

I think I'm leaving, Telemakos told his friends the rats, silently. Make a lot of noise.

But he was so cold he could not make himself move. The foreman got to his feet and joined the man who was already standing at the edge of the enclosure.

"Let's sweep the yard," he said. "You watch the walls; if there's anyone here, he'll try to go over. I'll get one of the dogs."

All right. Now.

Telemakos touched the small cut on his temple and assured himself he was not badly hurt. He crawled into the open yard away from where the men were sitting. The rain beat down.

The one who was scanning the walls never looked at the drains; he was looking for a grown man. Telemakos crept behind him, and had just reached the channel that would lead him out, when there was a shout from the foreman.

"Beware, Daken! The dogs have been drugged!"

Telemakos pitched himself headfirst through the teeming culvert. His arms and face plunged into stabbing spikes of desert thorn jammed flush with the outer lip of the drain.

Telemakos pulled back in panic, stripping his hands and wrists to ribbons. The bales of thorn had been moved closer to the building since he came in, probably before the meeting had started: the smugglers had foreseen treachery within, and had laid a trap outside the factory for anyone attempting to escape over the walls. Telemakos crouched at the opening to the drain, hidden only by darkness. The men shouted over his head. He slid out on his stomach, feet first this time, and tried to kick the thorn out of his way.

He emerged in what seemed a forest of it, like Crow in the story escaping from Fox: *Please, please, please don't throw me into the bushes!* Telemakos was not a crow. He could not open wings and fly free. He kicked and tore his way through the zareba, so cold now that he could not feel the spines ripping his bare legs.

Then he was out. He could hear the men calling to one another from within, and the noise of the one barking dog. They would use the other, the quiet one, to try to find him. Telemakos ran.

He was clumsy and slow. He was back in the street now, but he could hear the chase behind him. If this turned into a race, he was lost.

Hide, *hide:* they think they're looking for a *man.*

He got himself into the thatch of a roof somehow, and the hunt passed beneath him. It was too wet for the dog to pick up any scent. Telemakos waited, praying that Medraut had not been shadowing him this night, and taking back every ill oath he had sworn against the chance storm that was hiding him.

He was now so skittish he could not make himself walk down the middle of the street. He scuttled from doorway to doorway along the back alleys. If they chased him, if they followed him, there would be no sanctuary anywhere; even if he was able to outrun them, once he disappeared into the governor's house they would know who he was, or could soon find out. He had to escape unseen.

"What in God's name have you been doing, boy?" the governor's gatekeeper asked, agape.

"I had a fight with someone's dog. I was trying to cut home through the gardens in the merchants' suburb."

"You were lucky, Telemakos Meder," said the gatekeeper. "I know a man there who has trained bowmen guarding his villa. They shoot at you before they talk to you. You want to keep away from the merchants' mansions."

"I will," said Telemakos.

"Don't go in through the Domed Court. The archon's wife is giving a party."

Telemakos limped inside, leaving a trail of mud and thatch. His father was waiting for him in the entrance hall.

Medraut seized Telemakos by the shoulders and shook

him, and gave a voiceless sob and embraced him, and held him off and shook him again. Telemakos was beyond coping with his father's furious, desperate concern. He did the first thing he could think of to escape, and walked into the party.

The ladies stared and clucked. The lords joked and snickered behind their hands. "Is my mother here?" Telemakos asked the archon.

Abbas stared at him in disbelief. "Do you need a beating, boy?"

Telemakos glanced down at himself, wondering darkly, Do I look like I need a beating?

"My mother told me to greet her when I was safely in," he said levelly.

Helena, the archon's merry wife, pealed with laughter, and her friends with her.

"Turunesh, you shameful excuse for a niece!" Abbas roared across the hall. "Come and greet your wretched child!"

Telemakos found himself made to sit in a deep nest of cushions, with Turunesh on one side of him and Goewin on the other. Goewin's silken black hair was coiled up and crowned with a narrow tiara of pale Indian sapphires; Turunesh wore intricate bracelets of coral and ivory. Telemakos knew he must look unbelievably scruffy between them. "He hasn't been fighting," Turunesh said, waving concerned and curious faces away from them, her bracelets chiming. "It was a dog. He's crazy with animals. He naps in the emperor's lion pit. He's all right, he doesn't need a doctor, he needs a bath. Telemakos, my love, what do you need?"

"Coffee," he said promptly. "Hot."

Goewin and his mother threw back their heads and laughed.

"Yes, all right, love, coffee! Just this once. Helena, can we have a pot, a burner? It's late, I know—"

"Let me do it," said Goewin. "I love making coffee."

The ladies waited on him, turning his tattered and filthy state into a tremendous joke. It was marvelous.

"I should go to bed," said Telemakos.

"I shouldn't," said Goewin. "I should sit here drinking coffee and let the gentlewomen of Adulis fuss over my hair."

"Ugh."

"You should see to these scratches, though, my love," his mother said softly. "I don't want you dying of a dog bite gone septic."

"I wasn't bitten," Telemakos said. "I'll go in a minute. I'm still so *cold*." He pressed his side against his mother, and his back deeper into the cushions.

"I'll find someone to fill a bath for you," said Goewin. "I want to hear all about it."

ABRAHAM AND ISAAC

"Pour me barley in well-stitched leather bags,
twenty measures of meal, your stone-ground best.
But no one else must know."
2:391–93

IT TOOK TELEMAKOS two hours and a succession of hot baths before he was able to stop shivering. In the deep of night his mother, his father, and Goewin all crowded into his small bedroom as Medraut at last began to tend the slashes left by the thorns. Telemakos leaned against his mother's waist while she clasped his hands in hers, holding them back when he flinched and pressing them tightly when she thought he needed sympathy.

Medraut worked with a shapeless bar of salt in one hand and a bottle of some choking volatile spirit in the other. He scrubbed these alternately into Telemakos's torn arms and legs. There was no tenderness, no kindness in his work. He bent over Telemakos's ribboned hands with narrowed eyes, his lips pressed together in a tight, thin line. His whole body radiated anger.

Goewin helped her brother, silent as he. She was angry, too. Neither of them was angry at Telemakos; they were angry at each other.

When Medraut raised the bar of salt to begin work on his son's face, Telemakos sobbed and hid in his mother's shoulder.

He could not help it. He did not mean to. He was so tired. Medraut hesitated a single second, then took hold of Telemakos's hair and pulled his head around to face him.

Goewin said stonily, "Go to bed, Medraut son of Morgause."

Medraut let go of Telemakos's hair. Slowly, he laid aside the salt.

"Who—?" Telemakos dared.

"Morgause? His mother. Your grandmother. Queen of cruelty. Queen of evil."

Turunesh hugged Telemakos against her as Goewin and Medraut waged a strange, lopsided battle.

Goewin threw down the cloths she held and snatched hold of Medraut's left hand. The back of it was badly scarred; the last two fingers were stiff with arthritis. "Remember?" Goewin said. "Remember how she punished you? Don't do this to Telemakos." She turned Medraut's hand over and pointed to the blue serpent printed on his palm. "You are a doctor," Goewin said coldly. "Telemakos needs healing. He does not need punishment."

Medraut stabbed the air with a vicious finger, pointing at Goewin.

"Oh, you are punishing me already," Goewin snarled at him. "I will be sick if you make me watch this any longer. His wounds are clean. *Go to bed!*"

Telemakos slept in his mother's room, cradled in Turunesh's arms like a toddler, until he was warm again.

They would not let him out of the house until the scratches began to heal. After two weeks Telemakos grew bored. He sat on the floor at his mother's feet while Helena chattered about her grandchildren. Telemakos should meet them, Helena said; it would keep him out of trouble to have companions his own age. Telemakos sat on the floor at Goewin's feet, poring over the maps they had made together. He asked his father to show him how to use a crossbow.

He wondered about the Lazarus. He did not think it was any more real a name than the Authority, although both clearly referred to real people. The men in the mint had spoken the words as if they were titles in a special language.

"What is a Lazarus?" he asked Goewin.

"Someone who has escaped death. Lazarus is a man who dies and comes to life again, even from the grave."

"A ghost?"

"Not a ghost. A man alive. Christ restores him to life. It's in the Book of John, I think. I'll find it for you. Would you rather read Greek or Ethiopic?"

"Oh, Ethiopic, please."

Once Telemakos knew the story he could not get it out of his head. He was struck by how dearly the biblical Lazarus was loved, how his sisters and neighbors wept for him, how his friend Jesus went back to his aid even though it put his own life in danger.

"What on earth are you doing?" Goewin asked Telemakos, coming into the cartographer's office late at night. "We put you to bed two hours ago."

"I wanted to see if the Salt Road is mapped."

It was the third time in the week that he had started from sleep in terror. He had had his fill of lying in the dark, wide awake and quaking.

"It's nearly midnight, Telemakos."

"I keep dreaming about Lazarus, about the dead man when he comes out of the tomb. I hate that part. 'His hands and feet bound with bandages, and his face wrapped with a cloth.'"

He drew in a sharp breath, hearing his own voice speak aloud the words that were haunting him. "I cannot stop thinking about it."

Telemakos almost could feel his aunt's sharp, intelligent eyes boring into the top of his head as he bent over the unrevealing sketch of the Salt Desert. The page showed little more than a line of ink struck across fanciful lumps that might be mountains.

"But that is a moment of joy and wonder," Goewin said quietly, "not horror. That is the moment when his friend saves his life. Remember what Jesus tells them? 'Unbind him, and let him go.'"

Telemakos said, "I have an idea how to find him."

"Who?"

"The Lazarus."

Goewin said nothing for a long moment. Then she murmured, "Your father will not like this, will he?"

She slid the projection of Afar from beneath his hand. "Save it for morning, Telemakos." She gave his hand a squeeze. "There is a better map than this, but I will have to ask for it. It gives the landmarks and their alignment with the stars."

The monsoon was coming to an end. The winds were about to change. One day when the morning haze smelled of the sea, Medraut and Goewin stood near Telemakos in the archon's practice yard as he wrestled with his father's crossbow.

Goewin said in a low voice, "I want to send Telemakos to Afar."

It had taken Goewin a week to draw up the courage to speak to Medraut, Telemakos knew. But the winds would change any day, and then there would be no time.

"There is one man who is the key, the link in the illegal salt market. The smugglers call him the Lazarus. The only thing we know about him is that he's going to inspect the mines in Afar in the coming season. I want to send Telemakos to Afar to find him out."

Medraut gestured for her to continue. There were three hundred miles of desert between Adulis and Afar's distant borders. It was so impossible a journey that Medraut listened politely, incredulous at the suggestion of sending Telemakos across that barren country.

"He'll travel with a caravan, for his own safety, but not with their knowledge. He'll shadow them. They'll help him set a pace and find water, and show him the way. He'll have to carry his own water and any food he might need beyond what he can hunt."

Medraut stared at her as though she were insane.

"He'll have to wait at the quarry until this smuggler arrives, then return with another caravan."

Medraut stood as a statue, his brows lowered. He looked as though he might kill something if he moved. Telemakos had never seen him so tense.

"We won't do this without your permission, Medraut," Goewin said.

Medraut touched Telemakos's shoulder to make him put down the bow and stand still. Then Medraut held up his left hand to Goewin, so that she must look at the stiff, arthritic fingers and the scars across the back of his hand.

She shook her head in bewilderment, but said nothing, as though infected by his silence.

Medraut held his hand out to her, palm down.

"What do you mean?"

He pointed to the ruined fingers with his other hand.

"Morgause did that," Goewin said. "I reminded you, not long ago."

Medraut nodded assent, his eyes blazing, and turned away from Goewin a little, and pulled his shamma down over his shoulder to lay bare four ragged, pale scars like claw marks across his back.

"And that. I know!"

And then Medraut pulled the hair back from his neck to show her another set of claw marks, and he pointed to a tiny flaw in his cheek where the skin was shiny and smooth and his beard did not grow, and then he laid bare a terrible place along his inner forearm where his flesh had long ago been slashed and stitched and badly burned.

Goewin cried out, "I know what she did to you! I know what she did to Lleu! I know how inhuman she was! What has it to do with anything, today, here in quarantined Adulis at the Aksumite new year; what has it to do with Telemakos?"

Medraut took one of Goewin's hands, roughly and angrily, and laid it over the appalling scars on his arm. Then he took her other hand and laid it on Telemakos's head.

"Oh, *I would not*!" Goewin whispered. "I would not—I would not use him as my minion, I did that once, wrongly, and I swore I never would again. Not to coerce him, not without his willing consent—not for myself! Not to gain power for myself, as Morgause did Lleu! *As you did Lleu!*"

Medraut threw off her hands and turned away in a gale of fury. He pressed one fist against his forehead as if he were trying to stop his head from exploding.

"How can I make you understand, Medraut?" Goewin said fiercely. "I know how dear Telemakos is to you. God knows. He is dear to me as well. But we are battling *plague*. Telemakos may save all Aksum, if we let him."

Telemakos said in a small voice, "Ras Meder, I want to do it. I thought of it myself."

He touched his father's arm.

"I need you to take me into the wilderness," Telemakos said. "I need you to show me what to do, how to live. When you are sure of me, I'll go ahead on my own."

Telemakos picked his way to the window in his bedroom. The floor was piled with satchels, quivers, water bags that Medraut had specially made and tailored to fit a child, sandals, and shammas of varying thicknesses; three different bows were lined along the wall beneath the window. Telemakos knew which one he was going to take, but his father disagreed and had yet to approve his choice. On the windowsill lay flint and tinder, needle and thread, an assortment of small hunting knives.

"I'm not taking the flint," said Telemakos. "I won't be able to build a fire when I'm with the caravan."

"You take the flint," Goewin said firmly. She was sitting on the floor, weighing and testing the shammas. "I know you won't make a cooking fire, but if you get lost or hurt, fire may be your only way to call for help. Take it. It won't add much to your pack."

Telemakos moved the flint to one side, adding it to the list in his head. "Do you know what the smugglers call me? Well, not me, it's what they call the one who discovered the false sentries at Gabaza. They don't know it's me. They call me Harrier. I love that! And they have another name for me, do you know what they call me among the docks—"

Telemakos could not speak this aloud without laughing at

it. "I am— I am—" He leaned his face against the window frame, shaking with laughter. "The Python," he managed to gasp.

Goewin did not laugh.

"I, the Python!" Telemakos repeated. "Oh, go on, laugh."

Goewin said seriously, "It worries me to hear you mock them."

"It is funny, Goewin."

"It is, a little," she agreed. "But it means they hate and fear you, and I do not like that at all."

She looked up at him, then, and smiled a little. "Do you know what *we* call you?" she asked softly. "Gebre Meskal's special name for you is 'sunbird.' Little sunbird, so bright and energetic, so small it can hide in a flower. This will be my next message to the emperor: The sunbird is flying to Afar."

She touched the floor beside her. "My sunbird, sit here by me a minute. I want to talk to you."

He made his way carefully around the equipment spread over the floor and sat cross-legged beside her, his hands on his knees.

"Do you understand what they will do to you if they take you, and they think you are a spy?"

Telemakos closed his eyes for half a moment, his heart fluttering. What he thought of in that moment was not himself, but the black caracal: how it had stretched so languidly in the sun, flexing its mutilated paws, trying to knead the ground with claws that were no longer there.

He opened his eyes and answered in a low voice, "I think I do."

"I don't want to scare you," Goewin said. "But I don't want to betray you, either, by sending you all unwitting into hell. No one will treat you gently if you are caught. Only if they discover you are a spy, they will—they will deal bitterly with you, and show you no mercy. They will—" She faltered, her pale face oddly gray. She said abruptly, "They will break you open like a bird's egg."

Telemakos looked down at his hands. The thorn marks had nearly gone.

"Now, listen, Telemakos. You may be caught," Goewin said, her voice low and passionate. "You may be caught, but you must not be discovered, do you understand? No one must ever guess why you are there, or learn your name. Your hope will lie in making your captors think you are something else. An escaping exile, say, or a bond servant. I have thought hard about this, and if you will agree, I would like to mark you, in a way. You know your father's tattoo, how he uses it to tell people of his skill?"

She paused.

"Yes," he said.

"In Britain the Saxon invaders mark their bondsmen with a thrall ring, an iron band about their necks. My brother was so bound after the battle of Camlan, before he died. I want to band your neck like this, but in gold, not in iron. No one will know what you are this way, but if you are seen, they will know you are royal or royal property, and maybe that will make them think again before they harm you. I thought of just a gold chain or a torque; either of those would be easier for you to wear, but then it might look as though you had stolen it. This will have to be fixed on you at an anvil, and taken off the same way."

"All right," he said readily.

"Won't you mind?"

"It won't hurt, will it? Why should I mind?"

"It is a badge of servitude."

"It's only a disguise."

"It will not be a disguise," said Goewin. She clasped one of his slim brown hands between her white ones. "I am marking you as mine."

The winds changed. The new year brought Adulis the fresh air of the sea, blowing bright summer to the highlands.

His mother took Telemakos to the goldsmith's where the ring was fastened around his neck. No one but she could take him without attracting attention or being recognized. Telemakos had to pretend he was her servant. In truth, it was Turunesh who had to carry out the greater pretense, as she explained to the smith the nature of the work that was required; Telemakos himself spoke no word throughout the ordeal, except at the end, when he raised his head from the anvil and put up his hands to feel the thick collar that was locked about his throat. His mother asked then, in a low voice, "Does that hurt? Will it raise a blister? Is it too heavy?"

"I'm all right," Telemakos said, and knelt with his head bowed before her. "My lady."

Turunesh touched his hair gently. "Come then; let's go home."

In the dark before dawn on the day Telemakos left Adulis, Turunesh cut off his hair and carefully shaved his scalp clean. It was the last way they could disguise him.

"I wouldn't take care of it anyway," he murmured, thinking his mother needed solace.

"It will grow back," she answered calmly.

When she had finished, she kissed the top of his smooth skull. Goewin kissed him as well, on either cheek. Then she kissed the tips of her fingers and touched the gold band at his throat. "Ready?" she said.

"I'm ready."

Telemakos set out from the governor's house feeling strange and not himself, with the hard gold pressing at his neck and his head bare and sleek. Medraut paced silently at his side. They were southbound on the Salt Road before the sun rose.

In a way it was the most exhilarating outing his father had ever made with him. Medraut, testing Telemakos, let him do everything. Telemakos chose the way; he found the water; he set their camp; he caught their food. The land immediately south of Adulis was harsh and rocky, but not barren. Low acacia thorn trees grew everywhere, and reeds like grass, and aloe. Game was plentiful. The wayward rivers were full of catfish and crocodile. Even when the land grew less forgiving, Telemakos was still able to shoot tough little sandgrouse and occasional gazelle.

Telemakos and Medraut traveled a little away from the road. They would stay together as far as the last well before the Salt Desert, and then they would wait for a caravan, which Telemakos would continue with alone.

Once, coming to the top of a rise, Medraut shielded his eyes and pointed east. At the edge of the plain lay the first of the salt flats. White as the moon, dazzling as the sun, the salt stretched like a shining sea before a rim of jagged black mountains.

"It looks like snow," Telemakos said.

Medraut turned to stare down at him.

"It snows in the Simien Mountains sometimes. You can see it from Aksum."

Medraut ground his fists into his eyes to rub out the brightness of the salt. He touched Telemakos's shoulder lightly to set him walking again.

After a week they were well away from anywhere. All that told them this land was inhabited were the waidellas, the stone monuments to the Afar dead that littered the increasingly barren landscape. It was chilling at night. When dark fell, Medraut pointed toward the stars, and Telemakos told him their names and drew their paths in the dust, until Medraut was satisfied that his son was able to find his way by night as well as by day. In this empty place Medraut let Telemakos build a fire, and Telemakos was glad that Goewin had made him take the flint. He touched the gold band at his throat, remembering her kiss.

Telemakos was cold. He crouched by the fire with his

knees drawn up close to his chest, his hands in tight fists beneath his chin. Medraut held out an arm so that Telemakos might sit against his shoulder; Telemakos curled himself into the hollow between his father's arm and chest. Medraut pulled his shamma around them both, and Telemakos closed his eyes. Warm now, and happy in this wasteland with his father guarding but not guiding him, Telemakos fell asleep.

He woke in the deep of night to the sound of Medraut's voice. His father was muttering to himself in Latin:

"What makes you shiver so? Get up. You've no cloak. You'll freeze. Don't, don't, ah, don't cry. You cling to me so—do you still trust me, after all this?"

Telemakos could almost believe his father was awake. He was desperate, desperate for Medraut to be speaking to him. He wound his arms about Medraut's neck and whispered in his father's ear, "I have always trusted you."

"Little brother—" Medraut murmured, his voice anguished. "I can't. I can't kill you. I love you."

Medraut was not talking to Telemakos. Medraut was lost in a dead British winter with his dead British brother.

Telemakos buried his face in his father's shoulder and sobbed, very quietly, because it was so unfair. Medraut reached up to touch Telemakos's shaven head, as if to soothe him. The long fingers fluttered in bewilderment when they found no hair to gentle there. But Medraut did not wake up.

They arrived at the desert well and stopped for several days, hidden in a camp among the red rocks above the water. At last there came the caravan Telemakos was waiting for. He spotted the camels when they were still nearly a mile off, a train of black spots lurching against the skyline where the road crested a ridge.

"I'm going to fill my water bag before they get here," Telemakos said. He scrambled down the slope. The well was deep; you had to climb down a series of wooden ladders to reach the bottom. But the water was good, and surprisingly cold. Telemakos filled his skin and climbed back to Medraut.

They knelt and watched together as the caravan arrived. It was small, no more than fifty camels. The men climbed down into the well and tossed up jars and skins of water. They watered their camels, rested, built a fire, baked injera. At last they began to lead the camels on through the rocky desert. Telemakos waited until they were some distance away before he followed.

He touched Medraut's shoulder in farewell. "I'm going now," Telemakos whispered, although there was no need to whisper.

His father bent to kiss him on the forehead.

And then: "God go with you, Telemakos," Medraut said quietly.

Telemakos fell back on his heels, staring astonished at his father. He reached for Medraut's hands, but Medraut sank his face in his folded arms, leaning over one bent knee, and choked with hopeless tears.

Telemakos was suddenly cold and afraid.

"Ras Meder?" he whispered. "What did you say?"

"I said, God go with you." Medraut did not look up. "Go now, Telemakos. God provide for you. Go now."

Telemakos Alone

"So with Telemachus now. His father's gone.
No men at home will shield him from the worst."
4:183–84

IT WAS FOUR DAYS' journey before they found water again. Telemakos, unseen, slept with the camels. They were warm, if bad-tempered; they all lay with their knees bound together, hobbled so they could not wander off during the night. Telemakos could smell that one of them was in milk, and he sought her out. He was sorry to discover that she was nearly dry.

"Ah, bless you, sweet lady," he whispered almost soundlessly in her ear, gentling and coaxing her so she would not make a noise. She saved him one night's water. Even so, his small half-skin was empty by the time they made the next well. It worried him a little, but not much, because he knew the first reach was the longest.

He found the caravan's pace wearing. His legs were not as

long as a man's, or a camel's. The Salt Desert was below sea level; it seemed airless, until wind like a furnace raised a dust storm, and then you could not breathe at all. Telemakos thought it must be the hottest place in the world. Even his sweat evaporated without a trace.

The heat took away his appetite. He was not fond of raw meat in any case and ate very little. He knew he should eat more. But he could not force himself to do it when it choked him.

He felt as though he could never drink enough. He drank as sparingly as he could, and yet by the third well his water skin was dry again.

A day out from the well, he realized the skin was leaking.

It had happened so slowly at first that he had not noticed it. He had felt nothing, and the seeping water dried before it dampened anything around it. His camel had gone dry as well, suddenly but not unexpectedly; perhaps she minded the heat, too. I could go back, Telemakos thought, back to the third well, where there is water. But then he would be stuck at a well in the middle of the Salt Desert, with very little to eat and no water to travel with. If he went on, at least he was in company.

He decided to go on.

Thirst, killing thirst, crept up on him with the slow, relentless patience of a hunting cat, and took him all unprepared for its merciless grip. Soon Telemakos was pressing himself forward only because there was no alternative but to lie down and perish. One night and one day after his decision to keep going, he was barely able to stay close enough to the train of camels that he could keep them in sight. It was worse than that: he labored under the illusion that they were behind him. If he lost them beneath a rise, or behind an outcrop, he would turn around and actually see another caravan on the road at his back. When night fell, he sat shivering with his head in his hands, at a little distance from the camp, and tried to think.

I will have to surrender myself.

All that day he had veered away from admitting that this was his only and inevitable course of action. Now he shaped the words soundlessly with dry lips, to fix them in his mind: I have to surrender. I have to give myself up to these men, or I will die tomorrow.

Is that right? Think: Did I make the wrong decision yesterday; should I have gone back? That would have only dragged it out. I should have had to surrender myself to someone else, eventually.

He wavered, irresolute, sick with the thought of what surrender meant.

They will want to know where I came from. How I came here. There are no solitary boys wandering about in the desert; they will want to know my purpose. They will start asking questions, they will interrogate me, and if I make no answer they will—

They will break you open like a bird's egg.

He ground his fists into his eyes and shook his head and shoulders, forbidding himself to think any further ahead than the next taste of water. He no longer had a choice. He could scarcely open his mouth. He could not eat the injera in his pack. When he gazed out into the desert night, he imagined he saw the lights of a city shining in the distance; the gold bar ate at his swollen throat.

He knew, with bleak certainty, that he would die if he tried to push himself another day without water.

He broke his bow in pieces, and scattered them. He buried his knife, and the flint. His equipment was too well made, too well suited to himself; no runaway bond servant would be so aptly outfitted. He kept the water bag, and the pack with the food, so that his survival this far might have some credibility.

Telemakos lifted one hand to his throat and touched the gold collar, where Goewin had kissed it. Then he stole to the campfires and carefully chose the man who should be his savior.

The one he picked was calm and quiet, a camel man who took care with his animals and spoke to them patiently, as though they were children. This was no guarantee he would also speak patiently to a child, but it was better than no patience at all. Telemakos waited until the man opened one of his earthen water jars to take a drink himself, then crept to him quietly and touched him on the arm.

His mouth was so dry, and his tongue so swollen, that he could not speak. The camel man looked at him in astonishment, and Telemakos touched the jar. The camel man gave it to him without a word.

He took it away again a few seconds later, warning, "This is *my own water*, boy."

Telemakos stared at him, stricken, one pleading hand still reaching for the jar.

"Oh, go on," the man said grudgingly. "Don't drink so fast. Save some for tomorrow."

One of his companions called to him. "What the devil have you got there?"

"I am damned if I know," said the camel man. "Come look at it."

Telemakos put down the water jar and slowly raised his head.

He was caught.

"Thieving young crow, that's what it is," said one. "Look at that gold."

"It's fixed on him," said his rescuer. "He did not steal that. I'll tell you what he is: he's one of the emperor's nephews, or a cousin twice removed, or something like that. They always lock away the emperor's nephews so they can't try to overthrow him. There's a hermitage at Ophar, south of here, where he keeps them."

"I thought Debra Damo was where the princes are sent."

"This boy couldn't have come all the way from Debra Damo. It must have been Ophar."

The men looked Telemakos up and down. One of them reached for his empty water bag, and fingered it. "I think you're right," the man said through straight, white teeth. "But he could be a thief, too. He had to steal his tackle somewhere, did he not?"

"Go on and search him, then," said the camel man.

"Clothes off, boy."

Telemakos had not spoken a word throughout this exchange, partly because he had no place in it, and partly because his tongue still felt like kindling wood. Now it occurred to him that he should make these people believe he could not understand them.

"Clothes off, boy," White Teeth repeated.

Telemakos stared at the water jar as though it were the only thing in the world that mattered to him, which minutes ago had been true enough.

"Can he hear?" one of them asked.

I can't, Telemakos decided suddenly, I can't hear and I can't speak. I'm a deaf-mute royal brat, trying to escape the monastery where the emperor has sequestered me so my plotting relatives won't use me to seize the throne. I don't know what you'll make of my eyes when you see them in daylight—

They shouted at him in several languages while he blinked at them stupidly.

"He's deaf," said White Teeth with satisfaction. "Deaf and dumb."

It was a small triumph, a small unplanned advantage, to have succeeded in this deception.

They gave up trying to get him to take his clothes off and stripped him themselves. They were rough, and thorough, prying even into his ears and nostrils. They had no patience in trying to communicate with him.

"He's clean," said White Teeth. "But that gold necklace must be worth something. Can we not prise it off him?"

Naked and shaking with cold again, his body scathed by their invasive scouring, Telemakos knelt gazing blankly at their feet and willing himself to be submissive. Don't battle against them, he told himself; don't fight. I need their help. I have no one else. Their water will save my life.

"I'll tell you this," said the camel man. "He's worth a small fortune himself. Whoever put that band on him will pay its value, and more, to have him back."

Well, that's true, thought Telemakos. He would have touched the band again, for the solace it gave him, but they were talking about it, and he could not let them think their words had drawn his attention.

"What will you do, take him back to Ophar?"

"I haven't the time. Let's take him with us, and sell him at the mines; they can ransom him themselves. The warden there is no fool."

Well, that's just where I want to go. *Please, please, please don't throw me into the bushes!*

"He must not see the way. Cover his eyes."

Telemakos watched as they tore a strip of cloth from the long edge of his shamma to use as a blindfold, and unthreaded his sandal straps to bind him with.

It's all right, it's all right, he repeated in his head, over and over. If they cover my eyes, they won't be able to see them in the light of day, and that is another victory for me.

They fell on him like hyenas to a lion's leavings. They held fast his head, his throat, his arms and hands. They bandaged the torn piece of shamma tightly over his face, and fixed it in place across his eyes with a cord; then they wrapped the leather thongs from his sandals about his wrists, and attached them to another cord tied around his waist. Bound so, his hands were fixed loosely at his sides and a little behind his back, in order that he could not raise them to his face to try to free his eyes.

"Poor luckless rascal, look at him trembling," he heard his camel man say. "He doesn't know what's happening to him. Give him back his clothes and let him sleep."

"You dress him," said someone else. "You're the idiot who's going to share your water with him."

"I promise you he'll carry his share of my pack, as well," said the camel man. "Give me his goatskin. Maybe it can be mended. I've plenty of grease."

In darkness Telemakos was dressed again in his kilt and shamma, and led to a place where he could rest. In darkness he struggled to find a comfortable way to sleep with his hands bound by his sides; he was too cold to lie flat on his back, and ended in an awkward ball with his face against the ground and his hands behind him. Whichever shoulder he lay against went numb after an hour or so. In darkness he was pulled from sleep and given water, and some of the dried dates and salted meat from his own pack. In darkness his shoulders were laden with matting and sacks of flour, and one of his wrists was bound by a lead to a camel, and the caravan made its way slowly south.

Telemakos was barefoot now, as well as bound and blind. At the end of the day's march his camel man tore apart more of his shamma to use as bandages for his blistered feet. His mouth was so dry he could not moisten his lips; he could taste nothing, he could smell nothing.

But he was alive.

The men of his caravan were hard and heartless, but not corrupt. They knew there was a black market in salt; they were not part of it. They wondered about it. Telemakos knew a great deal more than they did, and knew he was safe with them, even if he was miserable.

He thought they traveled for a week. It was hard for him to tell, because being blinded made him lose all sense of time. They did not travel at night for the same reason they all went on foot, to spare the camels. So if Telemakos was too hot, and walking, it must be day; too cold, and resting, it must be night; but as they drew nearer the salt flats it grew so hot it was hard to track the difference. Telemakos arrived without knowing it at the encampment that served the Afar mines, and was sold without knowing it; only one evening his friend the camel man was gone, and Telemakos was led to a sleeping place among a line of silent, tired bodies who never spoke and never touched him. Their ankles were fettered one to another while they slept, like the camels.

So: I made it. I am here. I am listening.

Hara, the overseer at the mines, did not trust Telemakos at all. The wary, scheming warden was a man constantly waiting for his intrigues to be discovered, and he rightly suspected Telemakos to be something other than what he seemed. It was

Hara who insisted on keeping him blindfolded. He did not want Telemakos to see his face. Telemakos imagined him to have a pointed nose like a mongoose, which he poked suspiciously in everyone's business. He called himself Scorpion. Telemakos hated him.

The mines were manned by an odd mixture of convicts, a few of them exiled nobles, and free Afar and Aksumites of a handful of tribes. They camped at the well nearest the salt flats, a journey of some three hours each way. The men worked through the day's heat so the camels could rest in the night's cool. Every morning the men trudged on foot across the desert to the crusted lake where they cut and lifted the salt and shaped it with small hatchets into amole bars. Then they walked back to the camp. The camels were loaded with salt on the return trip; they could not carry enough water to sustain the men for more than a single morning's labor.

During the day Telemakos was set to ferrying water skins from the camels to the workers out on the salt. Fetching water was women's work, so no one ever wanted this job; at the mines it fell to those who had no other choice, and as long as someone loaded and led him, it was a task Telemakos could do without the use of his hands. He served the free workmen who could pour the water for themselves. To walk and stand among these men proved better luck than he had ever hoped for, for there was enough foreign traffic each day that even the Afar salt cutters spoke Ethiopic as often as they spoke their own language, and they talked unguardedly with one another as if Telemakos were not there. In a week he had pieced together the crimes and pedigrees of half the prisoners, and which of the foremen were not to be trusted and why, and the schedule of expected traders over the next three months.

This constant spring of information was his only consolation in an otherwise agonizing life of discomfort and exhaustion. His narrow ankles would not be held in a grown man's leg irons, so they were made to fit both at once through a single large shackle while he slept; then, hours before sunrise, Telemakos was led on the trek over the barren miles to the salt, and back in the infernal heat of early afternoon. The ring of gold seared his throat like a branding iron. His bare scalp grew sun-scorched, as did his nose and the back of his neck and the tops of his ears; when the sunburn blistered and peeled, the raw skin beneath burned over again. The cuts and open blisters of his first unshod march would not heal, but they were caked with salt now and did not fester.

Telemakos hardened to the daily journey. He did not doubt that if he failed to keep up he would be abandoned by the roadside, bound and blind and without water in the hellish desert sun; and maybe the Afar tribesmen would trouble to build a cairn over his desiccated body if they discovered him later. His deep horror of this doom pressed Telemakos more urgently than the whip that sometimes cut across the backs of his bare knees, and Telemakos kept pace with the miners.

All in darkness. In darkness he was led to the mines, in darkness led over the salt burdened with water he was never allowed to share, in darkness he was fed, in darkness led to the sleeping place. He hated the blindfold more than the goatskin straps that sawed at his shoulders, or the stale injera that was all they ever gave him to eat, or the hard salt crust burning the soles of his cracked feet, or the heat, or the constant thirst.

They never gave him enough water. For a fortnight or more he was given only three measures during the day's work—one before setting out for the salt flats, one on arrival, and one before the return trek—until he felt sure he would die within the month. He could scarcely feel his tongue; his lips were so dry they split and bled. If he wept there were no tears. When the empty jar was taken from his lips he yearned after it, as if the very scent of the warm, brackish water that had filled it could refresh him.

Telemakos and the one who held the jar for him were able to coordinate their movements so that no drop was ever lost. There came a light tap on the back of his head that told him the water was coming, and then the hand on his head held him steady, and the rim was held to his mouth: once when he was dragged from sleep, thrice during the wretched hours of blind labor, and lastly before he was pushed back down among the other resting bodies when the hours of labor were over. One blistering morning, the man who guided his drinking brought Telemakos an extra measure of water. Telemakos held still, feeling the priceless gift waiting against his chin; then he turned his head a fraction, and with his broken lips gently kissed the hand that held the bottle.

"Eh, you are welcome, boy," said a harsh voice, and another said, "He can't hear you."

"I forget sometimes," said the guide. "He's finer

mannered than any noble I've had in my charge."

How in the world can he tell that? Telemakos wondered. All I ever do is go where they push me and eat what they put in front of me. And I must look like a warthog when I eat, holding my bread between my knees and tearing it apart with my teeth.

"Aye, he carries himself like a young chieftain," said the other.

This worried Telemakos. He did not want anyone to notice him. He tried to seem more cowed.

It should have been easy. There was scarcely a shred left of his shamma, which they tore apart again to make a new blindfold when the first began to disintegrate. Telemakos had never imagined he could hate a lifeless piece of cloth as much as he now hated that shamma. Because of the blindfold Telemakos was kept bound; and that meant he could never sleep comfortably, nor feed himself, nor reach to adjust the water bags when they chafed his shoulders.

Nor could he stop them when they slipped.

Telemakos could carry one full goatskin, and that was a day's water for four men. It took all his strength to stay upright and stagger forward under this awkward weight, so to make better use of him his overseers usually loaded him with several partly emptied skins that could be evenly distributed over his shoulders. These they tied together into a makeshift harness, which one day came apart while Telemakos was waiting to be led out onto the salt.

He could not reach the slipping water bags, nor even see

where they were falling, but instinctively Telemakos swung around as though he had some hope of saving them. In doing so he collided with a man who was tying amole blocks to a camel's back. Salt and water came toppling down around them. One of the skins burst as it struck the ground, and Telemakos's sore feet were soothed with an unexpected wash of warm water even as he heard the salt blocks shattering.

He stood frozen while the amole crashed in a heap around his ankles. One of the falling blocks grazed his wrist bone hard enough to draw blood.

People surrounded him, cursing and crying out.

"The belt's slipped—"

"That is an hour's work smashed to ruin!"

"There's salt everywhere, man, who needs salt? The water wasted!"

Someone hit Telemakos across the mouth.

"Don't do that. You've no authority."

"Well, get Hara."

Telemakos stood waiting, filled with childish dread, while they fetched the vindictive warden.

Hara was brutal. "Careless whelp! Those bars were worth more than I paid for you!" He struck Telemakos again, driving him to his knees. "And who will go without the water spilled this day, young jackal's spawn? Eh? Too well born for work that any half-grown girl can do! Here in the desert he who cannot carry, cannot drink."

Telemakos cowered beneath the vitriol as much as the blows, and ground his teeth together in the effort not to answer in kind. All his hope lay in seeming ignorant.

Hara made a sound as though he were dusting Telemakos's touch from his hands. "Thunder and lightning, how am I to discipline a deaf-mute? Have this boy lashed. I hate these royal outcasts."

It was foully unfair. Righteous anger, and despair over the lost water, made Telemakos reckless. He fought as they untangled him from the fickle harness.

They bore down on him like hunting hyenas, with terrifying swiftness. Telemakos had nursed the illusion that although he volunteered his obedience, he was still free to move and object and make his own will known. But his will counted for *nothing*. He could not see to aim his blows; his feet and teeth never connected with anything, and his bound arms were useless. Every hand that touched him seemed twice the size of his own, and wielded thrice the strength. They overpowered him as easily as they might have held off a toddling infant, and much more cruelly.

They tore off his ragged shamma, and fixed his loosely bound hands tight together behind his back; then one of them managed to shove thick fingers into the scant space between Telemakos's throat and the band of gold he wore, and gripping the collar as though Telemakos were an unruly hound, the man heaved him across a stretch of burning gravel and hurled him against a wall of salt slag. Telemakos was so choked and stunned by this that he could scarcely breathe. He did not make a sound during the beating that followed, only because they did not release his throat until it was over.

When they let go of him at last, he sank to his knees, battling the need to weep aloud. After a little while this gave him focus, and he sniffed and sniveled abjectly in the blazing sunlight until his bonds were loosened slightly and he was set back to work. He was given no drink through all that afternoon.

Later, when he lay with his feet ironbound in the row of sleeping prisoners, Telemakos cried again, silently and to himself, for a long time.

No one will treat you gently if you are caught.

Telemakos did not mind hardship, and he was not usually afraid of being hurt. But he was beginning to thirst for kindness more desperately than he thirsted for water.

X

THE LAZARUS

—tight in his claws
a struggling dove, and he ripped its feathers out
and they drifted down to earth . . .
15:589–91

HIS HAIR WAS growing back. Telemakos could tell, because people suddenly began to touch his head, as if for luck, like the street children of Aksum. It came out of nowhere: when he was waiting for his shoulders to be hung about with water skins, when he was eating, sometimes when he was allowed a few moments to sit resting with his head against his knees between trips out to the salt. Light fingers brushed against his scalp and no one ever said anything. Eventually he could feel the slight give of the new hair as the surreptitious fingers swept over it.

There was not a thing Telemakos could do about his hair, except to hope that it would not be recognized or held against him.

Caravan upon caravan of traders arrived and left without

Telemakos's being parceled off to them, and he was in an agony of confusion as to what this could mean. Had they not been willing to pay whatever exorbitant price Hara asked for him, or had he not been offered to them? None of the bands had included the man Telemakos was waiting for, so he tried to be thankful that he had not been shipped off already. He suspected and hoped, and feared so cravenly he grew ashamed of himself, that Hara was waiting for the Lazarus even as Telemakos was, and meant to offer Telemakos to him and none other.

His tracker's intuition was dead on target. It was in fact more than two months since Telemakos had left Adulis, and a little less than two months since he had first come to the mines in Afar. Telemakos was one day stripped of his baggage and led to a place he had not been before, but which he knew existed: the enclosure where the foremen and warden camped. Telemakos was taken inside one of the shelters; he could tell he was inside by the shade, though it was not much cooler than without. It was anyway singularly different from the punishing legwork he had grown used to, and it set his nerves on edge.

"What is *that*?" said an oily, disdainful voice in accented Greek. "What is it?"

The man stank with a sour animal reek. Telemakos could not identify it, his sense of smell dulled by salt and thirst. It made him think of baboon.

The warden's voice answered, "I have an idea he is the one we call the Harrier."

I am *lost*, thought Telemakos in horror, and never moved.

"You are suspicious of everything," said the baboon.

"I am the Scorpion. That is my job."

"Scorpion!" the other repeated with deep scorn. "That is what you call yourself, at any rate. What makes you think this small, frightened thing is the emperor's most elusive informer?"

"Two reasons. One is that my own agents tell me the Harrier is no longer operating in Adulis; and the other is that in every caravan that has come from Adulis since the boy arrived, there has been some character asking about him, or offering to buy him, without knowing for certain he is here. One Afar band tried more than once. So I thought I should wait and show him off to you, before I sell him. Indeed, if you want him for yourself—"

Telemakos knew, in that moment, that he stood before the Lazarus. This was the man he had come to find. But the baboon, the Lazarus, could see him, and Telemakos could not see the Lazarus.

"Where did you get it?" asked the slow, disdainful voice.

"The first camel train from Adulis brought him. They picked him up on the Salt Road; he came to them out of nowhere in the desert, well on his way to dying of thirst, and begging them for water. They told me he is deaf and dumb, and he does seem so. They thought he was fleeing a sequestering."

"That white hair . . . " said the baboon, thoughtfully. "The British ambassador had hair like that, ten years ago and more."

Telemakos stood waiting passively, his heart thundering.

"They may be right about the sequestering, then," the baboon continued, still thoughtful. "None of the daughters of the queen of queens would want that bastard thing lurking about the New Palace while she tried to find a husband."

It made Telemakos want to laugh. It made him want to weep. His cursed hair might save him.

There was a noise of water poured, or beer perhaps, and the sound of the men drinking.

"If it's an imperial bastard I will have nothing to do with it." The baboon paused, and drank again. "I dare not draw attention to myself in Gebre Meskal's court. But if it is an emissary of his . . ." He spoke slowly. "If it is the Harrier, indeed I do want it."

Telemakos was beginning to feel sick with listening to these men toss his fate from hand to hand like a shining stone, while he must stand quietly pretending he could hear none of it.

"Why do you bandage its face?" the baboon asked then.

"The men he arrived with kept him blind so he would not learn the way, and I have kept him blind so he would not know me."

"That is a blindfold, then, not a bandage?" the baboon asked. "I should blind that thing for good, if it were mine, and have done with any fuss."

"He will be worth more whole."

"Blindfolds slip. My camel man could blind it for you very neatly. He does it with a pin; it scarcely bleeds. Or you might sew its eyes shut."

Telemakos had the impression that the man was trying to draw a reaction from him, and did not move. He had spent two months playing at being deaf and dumb; he was not going to let the fear of a threat betray him.

"I will not do that," said Hara firmly. "I do not dare that unless I know who he is. The Afar who tried to buy him insisted he is meant as a wedding gift for the bride of Ahamado, the son of their negus. They will not want him blinded."

"Well," said the Lazarus, "it is your own neck on the line. It does not know my name, Master Scorpion. But if it can hear, it most assuredly knows yours. Have you proof it cannot speak? Have you tested it?"

"The boy has never spoken. We whipped him once, and he did not cry out."

"Take this little knife and slip it between the creature's finger and fingernail. That will make it cry out, if it has a voice."

In his mind, Telemakos snatched frantically at images to hold against his heart, some way to endure and survive this test without making a sound; and his mind gave him again the caracal, stretching its amputated paws in the sun.

The warden said, "It is your knife."

"I will not touch that thing," said the Lazarus with disdain.

One of them, Hara, Telemakos supposed, gently took hold of his right hand. Telemakos stood still. He should not seem to know what was about to happen. He clasped the man's hand warmly in return, as though responding to affection.

The warden forced a sharp, thin blade beneath the nail of Telemakos's little finger.

Telemakos did not scream. He hissed in the back of his throat, like a cat, while the warden held firmly to his hand, twisting the blade as he pulled it out. Telemakos fell to his knees and sank his face against the ground, coughing and gasping.

The one who was the Lazarus said, "Do it again. Try the next finger."

God help me, Telemakos thought in blind panic, he is going to tear through all my fingers until I scream. And if I scream, I am lost, lost. They are so close to me, so close, and I am utterly alone—

The warden knelt by him and took up his hand again. Someone on the other side of the shelter broke into sobs.

The Lazarus snapped suddenly in Noba, "Yesaka, go outside if you must snivel."

Telemakos, huddled in a quivering heap and waiting for the next fearful test, was coolly aware then of two things. One was that the Lazarus was a native Noba speaker; and the other was that someone close by felt such pity for him that he was weeping. This seemed deeply important; this and the caracal.

"I wish you would do this yourself," Hara muttered.

"I wish the Authority would deliver the licenses himself," said the Lazarus. "But my childhood friend sits on the emperor's council, so he is above me, and I am above you. Test that thing again. Slice its nail off."

The warden prised up another of Telemakos's fingernails.

Telemakos fought. He spat and kicked and managed to sink his teeth into Hara's arm, and the knife tore a shallow scratch up the back of Telemakos's hand as the warden pulled away from him, cursing blackly in Ethiopic. Hara stood up and aimed a vicious kick into Telemakos's ribs. Telemakos choked and retched noiselessly at his feet.

The Lazarus sighed. "I suppose it *is* mute." He sounded relieved. "All right. Go on and sell it, if you like," he said. "But do not be fool enough to let it stay in Afar. Pack it off to Himyar with the next salt shipment, and it will never haunt you. I tell you this, Hara-called-Scorpion, if that thing sees me I will have its tongue cut out, whether or not it is mute, and its hands off too, and be damned to what it is worth. You would still be wise to glue its eyes shut, at the least. Use sugar paste or cosmetic jelly."

"Sugar paste!" The warden gave a bark of bitter laughter. "From my great unlimited supply of sweet almond confection, no doubt!"

"Use animal fat, then. Mix it with grit and splintered salt; then the thing will never dare to wipe its eyes."

"Yes, all right." Hara paced away and yelled in Ethiopic, "Minda! Get this mongrel's whelp out of here."

Footsteps came near him again. Minda, or another, put a hand beneath Telemakos's arm to encourage him to his feet. Telemakos refused to move. His collapse was real enough, but he was also desperate for some clue to the Lazarus's identity.

"Get up, boy!"

His name, his name, his name! The city where he lives,

the name of his house, the name of his wife, the name of his camel, anything!

"Minda, you donkey," said the warden, "lift him. He does not hear."

"You're right about it being royal," said the oily, disdainful voice of the Lazarus. "It's shiftless as a mule, isn't it? I expect it thinks it should be eating salt, like a millionaire, not cutting it."

Then in fury and hatred Telemakos very nearly tried to rub the blindfold off against the ground. If he could only see him, just once, he would know him again. One glimpse: It would be worth losing his tongue to be able to denounce this greed-driven, stinking sadist.

But the thought of losing his hands made him quail. He could not bring himself to do it. And while Telemakos hesitated he was dragged to his feet, led out of the shelter and away from the enclosure, and he could think of no reason why he and the Lazarus would ever be brought together again. He had failed. He was a coward, and he had failed.

He was made to sit and to wait, and then someone unwound the blindfold. Telemakos opened his eyes.

The salt was blinding. Everything was white. It was like staring into the sun. Telemakos saw nothing, nothing but the unbearable light, before he clenched his eyes shut against the pain and shock. Someone held his head still while another wiped handfuls of gritty, stinking grease over his face. Desperate, then, Telemakos tried to open his eyes again, but hard fingers pressed against his eyelids, and the fatty sand slipped between his lashes. Then the dreaded, hated cloth was wound about his head again. Another strip off his shamma was tied around his bleeding fingers.

"Did you see his eyes?"

"They're *blue*."

"He's a little goblin. I wish Hara would get rid of him."

That night Telemakos wept bitterly, as he always did before he slept, only now if he had any tears they were stopped by the filthy, stinging grease that matted his lashes together and glued his eyelids shut. He had come so close he could have touched the man he had been sent to find, and still he did not know his face or his name. Thirst and isolation were slowly killing him. And where were the emperor's other players, where were the ranks of chessmen Gebre Meskal had promised him, where was the army of warriors who would fight to defend him with their lives?

Telemakos lay bound and mute and blind, weeping without tears. His dry lips burned with the taste of salt.

XI

LIGHT AND WATER

"Let me go back to my own country now.
The heart inside me longs for home at last."
15:71–72

BEHIND THE BLINDFOLD, the grit worked its way into his eyes. They itched and smarted so incessantly that Telemakos thought he would lose his mind. He struggled against his bonds until his wrists bled, but he could not reach his face.

This torment became his whole world. He could think of nothing else; he lost all track of time. He lived in an infinite, isolate, lightless hell.

When he tried to figure afterward how long this lasted, Telemakos could never match his impression of it with the real time that had passed. It could have been as long as two weeks; it might have been as little as three days. It seemed to go on for months. But not long after the Lazarus's visit, against the Lazarus's advice, Hara sold Telemakos to the persistent band of Afar who wanted him as a wedding gift.

Again he was unaware that the transaction was being made, and he was startled out of the solitary, nightmare drudgery when he was effortlessly swung aloft in someone's arms and carried over a little distance. Telemakos did not give a blind damn where they were taking him. His knees and ankles had lately begun a persistent, piercing ache, echoed dully in wrist and elbow, which made it an immense relief to be given even a few seconds' rest.

"That young cur will never make a servant," Hara's voice commented. "He's already a runaway."

"Does he look like he's going to run?" the one who held him said curtly. "Well, if he tries, we'll send him back to you." Telemakos hung limp against the man's chest, steeling himself for another forced march.

But his feet never touched the ground again. His new owners did not free him, but they did not make him walk. They fixed him in a sling like a sack of flour on one side of a camel. The quirky rhythm of the camel's stride was curiously comfortable, and Telemakos slept through the first stage of the journey.

He woke when they lifted him down. Someone led him to stand on a carpet that felt like silk beneath his battered feet. He felt obsidian against one wrist, and then the other, as they cut away his bonds.

Telemakos stood still while it registered in his head: *My hands are free.*

He tried to raise them, and it was so long since he had

been able to lift them freely that at first they would not obey him. Then his hands moved without his telling them, clawing frantically at the cloth that still bound his eyes. He tore open his temple with a thumbnail in his desperation to be rid of the hated blindfold. At last Telemakos stood gasping with his hands pressed over his eyes, not daring to rub at them—they hurt too much—but just reclaiming them as his own.

"Get rid of that bandage," said a cultured, haughty female voice, in Ethiopic. "Ugh, I can smell it from here. Set it aflame."

Someone tried to pry his hands from his face. Telemakos fought, blindly and silently.

Get away from my eyes. Leave me alone, you hyenas, *leave me alone*!

They were stronger than he was. They always were.

They held his arms at his sides and made him sit. One touched the band at his throat, searching for a catch or seam in the metal. Another held his head still.

"Mother of God. Wash his face."

The rims of his nostrils, the corners of his mouth, the edges of his lower jaw beneath his ears were all crusted with salt.

One protested, "Water wasted—"

"No waste!" The girl's voice was imperial. "Look. Look what's been done to his eyes! *Wash his face*."

And someone did, very, very gently. It was done with such gentleness, and with such sober silence from those who must be looking on, that a green seed of hope opened and spread tender leaves in Telemakos's thirsting heart.

"Here, do this yourself, boy." A man was squatting by him; large, callused hands guided Telemakos's own to a bowl of water. "Rinse your eyes."

Telemakos's eyes were weeping and swollen, and he could not get the sand out of the left one. He hunched in deep concentration over the bowl, as though he would lose it if he sat up straight.

"Don't move."

The hard hands held his face still again, and there came the quick, invasive touch of a tongue between his eyelids, and the grit was gone.

The man grunted and stood up.

"He's lucky," the man said with satisfaction. "That could have blinded him, if he'd rubbed it in. Or killed him, if it had festered."

Someone else was kneeling before him, peering anxiously into his face. "Can you see?" asked the girl's haughty voice.

Telemakos had not uttered a sound for nearly three months, and was not about to give himself away at the first hint of gentleness that came along.

A soft hand touched his knee, and the girl said fiercely, "I have spent eight weeks in the desert negotiating a body price with toadying criminals. I have traveled back and forth like a peddler, three times, to those wretched salt mines. I chanced death should my intent be discovered, chanced worse than death! I will not now be ignored by the mangy mountain jackal whose freedom I was sent to buy. I want to know if you can see!"

Telemakos croaked in astonishment, "Sofya?"

"Peace to you, Telemakos Meder," she greeted him. "You've been lost."

To be spoken to directly, to be touched gently, to hear his own name again, were too much for him. Telemakos burst into tears.

"Can you see?" Sofya insisted.

"I don't know." He could not bear to open his eyes. "I think so. It's so bright."

"It will get better. Umar thinks your eyes are not damaged. How long were you held blind?"

"I don't know. Since before I came to the mines."

There was a long, long silence. No one spoke.

"Bound, also?" Sofya asked in a low voice. Telemakos did not answer. He lifted a hand to rub his nose. His arms felt leaden, but it was wonderful, wonderful to be able to move them at will.

"That white lioness you call your aunt will have my neck for not getting you out of there sooner," Sofya said darkly.

Telemakos remembered the night of the smugglers' meeting, and his father's fury, and how Medraut had held Goewin responsible for every scratch on Telemakos's body.

"Goewin must not ever know," Telemakos said, his voice unsteady. "Tell her *nothing* of how you found me. Tell *no one*."

He drew a deep breath. "It is enough that I was there."

"All right," the princess answered slowly. "I understand."

It took some time for Telemakos to adjust to being able to ask straightforward questions when he wanted to discover something. He could not shake the feeling of being hunted, of having to use silence and self-effacement to protect himself. Sofya's band of Afar warriors were naturally taciturn themselves, and only one of them spoke Ethiopic, so they did not volunteer information. Not until they had been traveling northward on the Salt Road for a full day, Telemakos swinging in his hammock at the camel's side, did it occur to him to ask, "Where is Esato?"

He had never seen one of the twin princesses without the other.

"She's the bride," answered Sofya. "She is wed to Ahamado, son of the negus over all the Afar. You're Esato's wedding present from the emperor."

"Am I?"

"Of course not, you featherbrain. Who would want a little gnome like you attending his bride? But we had to make some excuse for our interest in you."

"Why is Esato married, and not you?"

"Esato is my elder. She was born first." Sofya coughed. "I came with her, to see her wed. It is all she has ever wanted. She was very happy. She was beautiful."

Telemakos privately thought that all Esato ever wanted was to be as able and independent as her sister, but he did not like to say so.

Sofya added, "I shall not miss Esato, pulling at my clothes."

"Esato will miss you," Telemakos said quietly.

When he was awake, Telemakos was tormented with guilt and worry. But his sleep was profoundly untroubled. It was bliss to be able to open and close his eyes, to move his body at will, to lie still without his feet and arms going numb. He took to sleeping with his fingers hooked into the gold band at his throat. He longed to see Goewin again, more, he admitted guiltily to himself, more than he longed to see his mother. He was sure that Goewin's mark on him had saved his life.

After a week or so, Telemakos was able to sit astride his camel, and he could see well enough that he did not have to be led everywhere when he went on foot. It terrified him to think of how close he had come to being blinded. His left eye still burned and wept, though the swelling had gone down. Umar, the translator, tended him vigilantly. Umar wore an ivory bracelet above his elbow, which meant that he had killed at least ten men, so Telemakos submitted meekly to his care.

"Where are we going?" Telemakos asked suddenly, in the middle of another endless day of wilderness.

"Where else but back to Adulis?" Sofya answered.

"Has there been no plague?"

"Not in Adulis," Sofya said. "But we have lost our northern port, and the two coastal villages nearest it. We have lost Samidi."

They rode further in bleak silence. After a time Sofya asked, "Did you discover what you were sent to find in Afar?"

"I did not."

Telemakos looked down at his hands on the camel's reins, and at his maimed fingers.

"I did not," he repeated in a dull voice. He turned his head away so that Sofya would not see the silent tears brimming and seeping from his sore eyes yet again.

The world seemed very beautiful to him. Everywhere he turned, there was light: sunlight, moonlight, fireflies and firelight, lantern light and light on water, sparkling and moving; and water itself, river water, well water, spring water, water in tanks and stone-cut reservoirs. The taste of it, sweet and fresh once they were beyond the salt, left him gasping in astonishment. Even in failure and disgrace, these things captivated him. It was as though he were seeing and tasting them for the first time.

It was more than three months since Telemakos had started, when he and his escort reached Adulis again. Sofya sent Umar running ahead to tell the archon they would be there presently. The message brought Goewin dashing out to meet them.

"Telemakos! Telemakos!"

She raced across the busy market square, her skirts kilted around her knees, running like Athena. She waved wildly, shouting, "Telemakos!"

Telemakos threw himself from his camel's back, misjudged the distance to the ground, and landed in a heap in the street. He scrambled up and tore through the unheeding crowd toward her.

"Telemakos!"

He hurled himself at his aunt, leapt and flung his arms

frantically around her neck. She lifted him off the ground, and laughed and wept, her arms twined around his birdlike body so tightly it made him gasp. Goewin settled Telemakos on her hip like a baby, and Telemakos locked his legs around her waist to keep from falling. He leaned his head against Goewin's shoulder with his eyes closed while Goewin said softly to Sofya, "God's blessing on you, Princess. *God bless you.*"

Goewin kissed the top of his head and tried to put him down, but Telemakos would not let go.

"All right, I'll carry you," Goewin sobbed, still laughing and crying both. "You weigh *nothing.*"

Telemakos sobered a little and unhooked his legs from around her waist so he could stand. "I'll walk with you."

Goewin gave him a long, slow appraisal, up and down. Telemakos quivered to think what her dark eyes were tallying: his swollen face and flaking skin, sores at the edges of his mouth and nose, his wrists torn raw where he had strained to free his hands, and so and on. Goewin said firmly, "You will not walk. You shall climb back up on your noble camel and spare those unfortunate feet. I'm sure we sent you off in shoes."

Telemakos obeyed her as meekly as he had obeyed Umar.

Helena, the archon's wife and Telemakos's great-aunt, was waiting to make a fuss over him. For the rest of the day Telemakos let people pet and baby him. But they were not the people he had been longing to see.

Where are my parents, he wondered.

His welcome by the archon's household seemed frenzied and excessive. Helena kept breaking into sobs when she looked at him; one of Helena's young attendants ran out of the room to be sick when she saw the remains of his fingernails. They took too much care with him, and not enough.

Where are my parents?

All the attention tired him out more than the last day's camel trek, and Telemakos went to bed while it was still light. Goewin came to perch at the edge of his cot as she had done all through the monsoon season.

"Peace to you, dear one," she said. "You look exhausted."

"I'm all right," Telemakos said.

"You would say so. You mean you've not got plague, or been permanently crippled. What happened to your eyes?"

"They don't like dust. There's a raging sandstorm every afternoon, the Afar call it the 'fire wind.' It doesn't seem to bother them."

Goewin took his hand in hers, his right hand, and held it gently, taking great care not to touch the tips of his injured fingers. But she traced the knife's trail etched over his knuckles and up his wrist, a hairline scab like a strand of crimson thread clinging to his brown skin. "How did you come to be taken?" she asked in a low voice.

"My water bag leaked, and I had to surrender myself. I was— I would have died of thirst, I was already dying. I was seeing things that weren't there. I buried most of my gear before I went to the caravan, and tore my fingers up scraping in the rocks, but I didn't even notice I'd hurt myself till after they'd given me a drink. I had to ask for help. I would have died."

Telemakos produced this glib half-truth without any forethought. Goewin sat with her head bent, looking down at his thin hand, and if she noticed that the wounds could not be three months old she did not say anything.

"Goewin," Telemakos asked, "Where are my mother and father?"

"Oh, Telemakos, I am so sorry! I should have told you hours ago, but I've been waiting all day to have you to myself. I did not like to tell you with all Helena's ladies-in-waiting fluttering in attendance. Your parents went back to Aksum."

"Why?"

She was so indirect in her answer that Telemakos suddenly feared one or both of them must be dead. "*Why?*"

Goewin opened her mouth and closed it again, like a fish. Then she hit her head with the heel of her hand. "Mercy on me, why is this so hard?" she burst out. "Your mother—your mother is expecting a baby."

"Goewin, you jest!"

He could see that she did not. Telemakos laughed and flung his arms around her neck again. "Truly? My mother and father *together?*"

"Telemakos, you wicked child, of course your mother and father together. Goodness, are you really so pleased?"

"It's the best thing I've heard in months!" That did not

seem to do it justice, considering the last three months. "In years. The best thing ever."

"They thought—well, who knows what Medraut thought, but your mother thought you would not like it. She thought it would seem as though she already counted you for dead, and needed to replace you. She was torn apart at the thought of your coming back here and finding her gone. Oh, the battles! Turunesh would be too heavy to travel before next winter if she did not go now, and she was ill, the heat and the mosquitoes were making her miserable. She did not want to go. But Medraut and I both thought she should—can you believe that Medraut and I were in agreement?—so he took her back to Aksum."

"What did he say?" Telemakos asked.

"What did he say?" Goewin sounded perplexed. "What do you mean? He didn't say anything. He never does."

"I thought . . ." Telemakos sighed. "Never mind. I just hoped . . ."

"I know," Goewin said gently. "But he didn't. Though he has been so unhappy this season. In truth, I think neither one of your parents could bear waiting while train after train arrived with no sign of you—and then the word you must be captive—and Medraut could not go to you because anyone seeing him would guess who he was, and who you were—"

Goewin held Telemakos off. She asked softly, "Was it worth it?"

He found himself struggling against tears again. He swallowed, and managed to speak aloud the news he had been dreading to tell for so many weeks:

"I could not discover the Lazarus."

Goewin grimaced a very little. Telemakos swallowed again, and could hardly talk around the choking ache in his throat; but once he began he could not stop.

"I never saw him. I knew he was there, I knew it was him, but I never saw his face or found out his name. I keep trying to remember things about him, to puzzle it out, and I can piece together nothing. He sneered all the time when he spoke, he spoke through his nose. He did not like to touch anything. He smelled like a baboon. And he was cruel. He wanted to cut off my hands."

"You said you never saw him!"

Telemakos saw how close he was to betraying himself. "I didn't see him. He knew I was there, and he said that if I saw him he would have my tongue out and my hands off."

"My dear one," Goewin murmured, and pulled him against her, holding him close. "There," she muttered over his hair. "It was not done. It's over."

"You don't understand," Telemakos said, and it suddenly occurred to him that he could confess his failure to Goewin, that in fact he owed her his confession. "I could have seen him. But I was too much afraid, I knew he would have my hands off if I learned who he was, and I was too much a coward to risk it. And now we shall all die of plague because I was not bold enough to look on someone's face."

Telemakos turned his own face into Goewin's shoulder and sobbed.

"Child," Goewin said sorrowfully, "do you think for one moment I would have been better pleased had you returned to me with arms ending in bloody stumps, than I am to have you back whole and safe? Telemakos?"

She held him tightly while he wept.

"How could you get close enough to smell him and not see him?" Goewin whispered, and Telemakos could tell that she knew he was hiding something. What could he tell her to put her off—what else could he remember about the Lazarus—

"He was Noba. He said something in Noba to one of his attendants, and his accent was exactly like my Noba tutor's, like Karkara's. Karkara's stories are always of his Noba childhood—

"*Oh!*"

Telemakos untangled himself from Goewin's clasp so he could see her. "*It's Karkara!*"

She gaped at him. "The Lazarus?"

"Not the Lazarus, the *Authority*! It's Karkara! Karkara has been issuing the authorizations!"

Goewin's eyes widened with understanding, and she let out a long, low breath. "The devil! It is Karkara, isn't it. I can see it. Oh, Telemakos, well done, *well done*!" She reached impulsively for his hands again, and kissed them. "Oh, you are a bold hero! How did you leap to it?"

"It was something the Lazarus said, that his childhood

friend sat on the emperor's council, and there are no other Noba on the council. I did not remember it before, I was—I was not listening carefully when he said it—" Telemakos shook his head. He was coming too close again, and too close to more tears. Goewin could get the truth out of him if anyone could, and he must not tell her.

She was still holding his hands. "Telemakos," she asked quietly, in a low voice full of unhappiness, "did they hurt you, my love?"

He hesitated.

"They made me work. They whipped me, once, but that was because I spilled a skin of water and ruined a load of salt blocks—"

Only it was not his fault, and he had been able to do nothing to prevent it, and it had been the cruelest beating he had ever taken.

"They did not feed me much, and I was always thirsty—"

He had thought he was going to die. And the humiliation: being pulled like a dog by a lead looped through his gold collar; not being able to clean himself; the warden spitting on his bread.

And the unspeakable *loneliness*.

"I was lonely," Telemakos said. "I was so lonely. That was the worst thing about it." And it was.

Goewin sighed. She said, "Telemakos, I want you to go home. Sofya will take you. I can't leave yet, but I will follow as soon as I am able. Your mother asked me to send you back to Aksum when I could. You should be with your mother."

Telemakos said, rather plaintively, “I don’t want to go home.”

“For God’s sake, child. Why ever not?”

“I haven’t finished. I want to find the Lazarus.”

“Telemakos. Haven’t you had enough already?”

Miserably, he broke into another torrent of tears.

“It’s not enough. It’s not enough. Even knowing the Authority is not enough. The Lazarus will carry on without authorization. He doesn’t give a hang about authorization, it just makes his work easier. I have to find *him*.”

Goewin remained calm. “Karkara will tell us who he is. I forbid you to creep into another den of thieves until you weigh as much as you did before you started. I want to believe you were not hurt, but any fool can see you’ve been starved.”

Her voice went soft and sorrowful again. She laid a hand against his cheek. “Telemakos, you look like a ghost. So thin. Your skin’s gone all cracked and dull. Your body is covered in ugly little sores. I want you to go home.”

Telemakos sniffled and did not answer.

“Someone must tell Gebre Meskal about the Authority,” Goewin coaxed. “Shouldn’t it be you? I sent him my message this morning.”

He rubbed gingerly at his eyes. “Which message?”

“‘The snare is cut,’” Goewin said softly. “‘The sunbird flies free.’”

Telemakos sighed and laid his head against her arm once more. Her sleeve was damp where he had sobbed into her shoulder five minutes ago.

"Hush, my young soldier," she whispered. "Hush, you have done your work so well. Don't think about it anymore tonight." She rocked him gently, crooning praise over the stubble of his hair. "Hush, my brave one, my great one."

Telemakos sighed again.

"All right," he said at last. "I will go home."

He was back in Goewin's arms now, and the loneliness melted away.

SANTARAJ

"A pinch of salt from your own larder . . . "
17:503

TELEMAKOS STOOD WITH his head back and his hands linked behind him, staring up at the night sky. Sofya's entourage had pitched their first camp, one day's journey from Adulis, and Telemakos was supposed to be asleep. He had tried to settle in his sheepskin rug under the canopy they had tied up for him, but the smell of the nearby mountains was too exciting. It held a hint, only a hint, of coolness, and tall trees; of wild coffee and juniper, and rivers that ran yearlong. Telemakos had not known how homesick he was until he caught the faint scent of highland Aksum.

He stood looking up at the deep sky, in tears again. It maddened him to have done so much weeping since his rescue. The smallest things set him off.

"You are supposed to be in bed," Sofya said over his shoulder.

"I know, but the stars, so many stars, I can't stop looking at the sky. I have not seen stars for three months! I forgot about stars."

"You are going to have to do better than that," Sofya said. "'I forgot about stars'! People will think you've been entombed for a season."

Sofya was a good traveling companion, in spite of her ill temper. Half the talking she had ever done had been on Esato's behalf, or to explain Esato, or to make excuses for her, or to tell her off. With Esato gone, Sofya spoke only half as much. She was still congenitally sarcastic and insulting, but Telemakos thought most of this was habit; her heart was not in it. She watched him sharply, all the time. She would call the party to rest if she saw him flagging, but she never drew attention to his frailty. Telemakos thought he must have become a kind of substitute for Esato.

He tired quickly. He tired so easily he could not understand how he had managed to drive himself through the last weeks of his captivity without collapsing. The journey up the switchback mountain roads to Aksum was slow because of him, and it frustrated him deeply. How many villages were left on the northern coast—how many soldiers could Gebre Meskal continue to employ in shielding them—how long before some stricken individual escaped and made his way to Adulis, while the disdainful baboon sat on his growing pile of tainted gold—

"Don't imagine you're going to bring down the black market in salt all on your own," Sofya remarked one day, "or by yourself enforce the emperor's quarantine. Aksum's fate does not rest entirely on your bony shoulders. Gebre Meskal does have other servants. Stop sulking."

"I'm not sulking," Telemakos said.

"You sit on your pony glowering like a vulture all day long."

"I don't. I look at everything. I count the antelope. I saw twelve different kinds, yesterday. And the trees! That one late blooming kosso, did you see the beautiful red flowers this morning, among the deep green?"

"You are more bearable as a holy innocent than as a sulking vulture, but only by an eyelash," Sofya said. "What a task to set a child, cross the Salt Desert alone and break up a smugglers' ring!"

"I could have done it," Telemakos said, and he was sulking. "It would have been easy if I'd had a decent water skin."

"Your aunt should be strung up by her toenails."

"Do you shut up, Woyzaro Sofya," Telemakos said hotly.

He never stayed angry with her. He could not argue with her hard, careless honesty. He liked it. It was much better than Helena's pitying glances, or his father's silent fury.

They came at last to Grandfather's villa in Aksum. Telemakos stood in the street outside the gate and said, "Will you come in? Stop and have your meal here before you go on."

"I think we should let you go alone," Sofya said. "Your grandfather is not expecting visitors."

"Thank you, Sofya—thank you for all," Telemakos said. He did not have the words to thank her adequately.

"Gebre Meskal does have other servants," she repeated

loftily. "Now go and let your mother lick your wounds, you sorry little mountain jackal. Come and talk to me at the New Palace if they ever let you out again."

Telemakos went through the gate.

Ferem was lighting the lamps in the forecourt. He set down his taper and kissed the boy on either cheek. "Telemakos! Welcome, dear child, welcome to your home. Turunesh said you were too gravely ill to travel—we did not expect you! What's happened to your hair?"

"They cut it off when I was in fever," Telemakos said.

"Come inside. Your mother will be overjoyed."

Telemakos ran up the steps two at a time.

Turunesh was not noticeably bigger, but her eyes were shadowed with indigo rings, like bruises against her dark skin. Her face was thin. Telemakos wondered if these were the marks of illness or of worry or of carrying a child, and decided it was all three.

"You've been lost! You've been lost!" he cried, and threw himself at her.

"Peace to you, Telemakos Meder," she breathed over the top of his head, and held him tight. After a little while she laughed softly, and said, "Go take a bath."

Telemakos woke in his mother's bed, alone. He had slept late into the morning. He could not seem to sleep enough; it was as though his body were making amends for the hundreds of hours of sleep it had recently lost.

Turunesh had left out clothes for him. Telemakos tried to fasten his kilt strings as usual, and gave up; he was too thin. He had to tie a knot in the fabric. He padded to the window and looked out at the sunny courtyard, at the empty niches in the white walls where the doves used to live. He could not believe he was home.

Paradoxically, he could not believe he had ever been away. It seemed so natural, so ordinary to be here; Afar could not have been real. Telemakos crossed his mother's bedroom to gaze at himself in one of her bronze mirrors, and the proof was before him: the gold bar at his neck, scratched and dented; his short hair haloing his face with light, as though he had wiped his scalp with sea foam; his lips still cracked and peeling; one eye still shot with blood, though no longer swollen. Telemakos knelt at the dressing table with his chin resting on his folded arms, staring at his strange reflection. He saw his mother come up behind him, and she ran her fingers lightly over his bristling head.

"Your hair needs oiling."

"I told you I wouldn't take care of it."

Turunesh laid her hands gently over the fading marks on his bare shoulders, where his skin had been chafed and cut by strap and whip.

"What did you do in Afar?" she asked.

"I was a water bearer."

"Do not the Afar women do such work?"

"There weren't any women at the salt mines."

She touched his collar and said quietly, "Come with me to the jeweler at the New Palace. It's time you were freed of this shackle."

"Not yet," Telemakos said. "I haven't finished."

"Sweet heart, you're home; it's over."

"I haven't finished," Telemakos repeated.

That afternoon he went to the New Palace on his own, in search of Gebre Meskal. Sofya must have told the emperor they were back, but Telemakos was still not sure how he would manage to get Gebre Meskal alone; he found, to his dismay, that the mere thought of hiding himself now exhausted him.

Telemakos sat idly on the rim of one of the lily pools in the Grand Hall and messed about with the water. Like sleep, he could not get enough of it.

Maybe I can just lie in wait here with the other courtiers until Gebre Meskal sees me, Telemakos thought. If he sees me, he will send for me.

Another saw him first.

"Telemakos Meder."

Telemakos looked up, then stood quickly. Of all men, of all men in the Aksumite imperial court, it was Karkara.

"Where have you been these long seasons, Telemakos? Your lions have missed you."

The councilor had never treated Telemakos with anything but absentminded kindness. It had always seemed to surprise Karkara when Telemakos turned up in his office.

But Esato had been afraid of him.

Telemakos frantically shook the water from his hands. "Adulis," he answered, ducking his head respectfully as Karkara wiped drops of water from his face. "I was in Adulis. I stayed with my grandfather's brother, Abbas the archon. His wife, Helena, is very sweet to children."

"I visited Adulis myself not long ago," said Karkara. "I did not see you there."

"I've been ill," said Telemakos.

"Are you better now?"

"Much."

"Then you will have to take up your lessons in Noba again," said Karkara.

Telemakos, who had been gazing at the elder's feet, dared to raise his eyes.

"I do not think I shall need any more lessons with you," Telemakos said, and lowered his eyes.

"Insolent young scoundrel," Karkara scolded mildly. He cuffed Telemakos lightly on the shoulder. "If the emperor wants you to speak Noba, so you shall."

"I beg your pardon." Telemakos pulled his shamma back into place, and Karkara suddenly laid two careful fingers against the gold at Telemakos's throat.

"What is this?"

"A present from my aunt," Telemakos said. "It's a Saxon necklet, like they wear in Britain. Goewin took great care of me when I was ill."

"You are lucky in her," Karkara said. "I will speak to the emperor about your lessons."

"Will you see him soon?" Telemakos asked. "Will you tell him a thing from me?"

Karkara gazed down at him with weary amusement. "All right, then, Telemakos Meder. What is your message?"

"His tame sunbird has got into my grandfather's garden," said Telemakos, "and as the emperor knows, it will answer to him and none other."

"I did not know Gebre Meskal keeps a tame sunbird," said Karkara.

"You do now," Telemakos replied coolly.

Medraut was waiting in Grandfather's garden court. Telemakos bore squarely his father's shrewd, critical scrutiny. More than a month had passed since Telemakos had been freed, and though he was not fully himself again, he knew he no longer looked as if he had recently been buried alive. Medraut held an arm open to his son, and when Telemakos ran to sit by his side, Medraut put a small parcel in his hand.

"What is this?" Telemakos asked. Oh, he thought, what a stupid thing to say, of course Ras Meder won't tell me what it is!

Telemakos unwrapped the leather bindings. It was a sheaf of unbound pages covered with dense, precise script. Telemakos glanced at the first page and turned the leaves over with growing delight. Medraut had given him a copy of the first four books of Homer's *Odyssey*, but in Ethiopic, not in Greek.

"The *Telemakia*! The voyage of Telemakos!"

The script was unadorned, in flat black ink, but certain words among the text stood out in sudden violet in the middle of one page: "Telemakos," and "a darling only son."

There was no inscription other than these few of Homer's words picked out for emphasis. Telemakos stared down at the small, painstaking script.

"You wrote this out yourself! You translated it yourself? For me!" His father had only ever given Telemakos a handful of words in his life, and here was an entire book of them.

Telemakos began to cry again.

I must stop this, he told himself sternly, sobbing into his father's shoulder and clutching the priceless pages against his chest. I weep at everything. What did Sofya tell me: You are going to have to do better than that.

He made his mother read the whole thing aloud to him over and over. He loved to hear his mother's voice speaking the words his father had written, and he loved hearing his own name in a heroic fiction. Telemakos was listening at his mother's feet, late in the afternoon, when Ferem came in to them and said, "The ambassador is here. She traveled partway with an official from Tekondo; Kidane has invited her guest to dine with him. Their party is unpacking in the stable yard. Shall I bring them in?"

Telemakos scrambled to his feet and ran to meet Goewin.

He put one foot down the forecourt stairs and stopped, frozen in place as if he had been suddenly stung by a scorpion. For several seconds Telemakos had no idea what was wrong with him. Something had made him recoil in hopeless terror;

he found himself crouched trembling against the stair wall, his head up like a hunted gazelle, sniffing the air. He could smell nothing unusual: frankincense from the plantation on the hill, and the horses in the stable. But again, there was something else, faint. He caught it and broke out in gooseflesh. It was a rank stench like baboon. It was the stench of the Lazarus.

Only it was not baboon. The strange smell came to him once more, a little stronger. It was like baboon, but it was something else. Telemakos turned his head this way and that, trying to catch the scent. Every time it came to him he clutched his arms tighter around his knees and hugged himself closer to the wall, cold with fear and evil memory. It was the Lazarus, without a doubt, but it was not baboon—

It was caracal.

His mind had known all along, without being able to piece it together. All the while as he had stood before the Lazarus in Afar, his mind had offered him the image of the caracal, and he had not known why until this moment.

Goewin led her guest out of the stable yard and across the forecourt. There at her right hand was Anako, Deire's conniving archon. The black caracal and familiar, sullen, moustached boy followed at their heels. Anako: he looked like any official, his hair running to gray, his body running to flesh. His heavy hands were bright with gold rings.

How can it be Anako? Telemakos wondered. I thought Anako was dead of plague.

But he isn't. That's why he's called the Lazarus.

They came up the stairs to the house, and there was Telemakos cowering underfoot, his white hair shining in the afternoon sunlight, the broad gold band glinting at his throat.

Anako gazed down at him with bright, contemptuous eyes. Telemakos hid his face in his arms.

"Please, go in and I will follow," Goewin said to her guest. "Kidane will be waiting for you in the reception hall."

"Thank you, lady," said Anako in that hated, disdainful voice, and he continued up the stairs. Telemakos huddled on the steps without looking up while they passed.

Goewin crouched by his side. "What's wrong?" she hissed. "What is it?"

Telemakos whispered, "It is he. It is he."

"How do you know?"

"He stinks."

Telemakos raised his head and gnawed at his knuckles, staring into the distance.

"He is unpleasant, I'll grant you that," Goewin whispered fiercely. "I have detested traveling with him. But Telemakos, you can't accuse a man of treachery because you don't like the way he smells!"

Telemakos shook his head. He chewed at his fist. Then he whispered through his teeth, "Let me wait on them. When he has supper with Grandfather, let me wait on them. I'll do something stupid, drop a jug or spill something, and Grandfather can go out to get Ferem to help clean up. Leave me alone with—with *him*—for half a minute."

"Why?"

"He'll try to kill me. Then you can accuse him of treachery."

This time Goewin hissed through her teeth without speaking.

"Half a minute, no longer!" Telemakos said.

"All right," she whispered. "I must go." She squeezed his hand tightly.

Telemakos still stared into the distance. "He thinks I can't speak, or hear. Tell Grandfather."

Goewin stood up, gathered her skirts, and ran into the house. Telemakos sank his face into his arms again and sat shivering in the sun for another minute. Then he forced himself stiffly to his feet and followed the others inside.

His body slipped easily into the habit of dumb stupidity. He did not have to pretend to be clumsy, waiting at Grandfather's table. Telemakos kept his eyes fixed on Kidane so that he would not have to look at the other man who ate there also.

"How did you come to escape the destruction of Deire?" Grandfather asked Anako.

"I was on my way back when it began. The cordon was in place before I arrived, and I was not allowed in, so I returned to my estate at Tekondo. I reside there now. But most of my business is in Adulis or Aksum; I still do trade in salt." Anako paused, as Telemakos opened the mesob basket to take out the injera and lay it before them.

"Do you know, I am still named Deire's archon," Anako added. "I am a governor without a city."

Grandfather chuckled.

Grandfather was wonderful. He never said a word to Telemakos; indeed, he scarcely looked at him, but pointed and gestured to the things he wanted Telemakos to fetch, as if there had been a deaf-mute servant in his household since the beginning of time.

Telemakos spooned wat over the injera.

"I should like to salt this meat, if I may," said Anako, and Grandfather pointed Telemakos to the salt.

I'll give you salt, thought Telemakos.

He cut a tablet from the bar on the wall shelf. *I expect it thinks it should be eating salt, like a millionaire, not cutting it.* Telemakos knelt, to work with the black granite grindstone between his knees, holding it so tightly his wrists began to ache.

I'll. Give. You. *Salt*, Telemakos thought, pounding the tablet to splinters, and then to dust.

You called me a thing. You called me "it" as though I am not human. You said to slice my nails off. You wanted to sew my eyes shut.

The powdered salt spilled over the floor like ash. Anako stared at him. Telemakos drove the grindstone into place once more, and the salt mill came apart in his shaking hands.

XIII

The Harrier Stricken

Now there was an ambush
that would have overpowered us all—overpowering,
true, the awful reek . . . !
4:495–97

TELEMAKOS STOOD UP and set the chipped grindstone on the basket table before Anako, and also the split halves of the granite bowl. He knelt again and tried to sweep the spilled salt together with his hands.

Grandfather rose quietly. "Please forgive the child. He was very sick earlier this season, and it has made him awkward. Do you excuse me; I'll get my butler to sweep that up." He left the room, and pulled the door shut behind him.

Telemakos knelt fixedly brushing the salt about on the floor, not daring to look up.

Anako remained quite still, as though lost in a dream. Then he picked up the grindstone with one hand, and a broken piece of the mortar with the other. He weighed and stared at them as if they held some kind of secret meaning that he was trying to conjure.

Come on then, Telemakos willed him. Give yourself away. You know who I am.

Anako got to his feet. He bent over Telemakos, and without any warning brought the heavy pieces of stone crashing down over the boy's temples.

Telemakos heard the blows as great, deep gongs ringing inside his head, and he fell like a bird shot through the heart. He felt nothing. His world went black for half a second, but then he was wide awake again, his mind clear and alert; only he lay flat on his back and could not move.

Anako spoke to himself, or perhaps to Telemakos, in a low, monotonous stream of nervous self-justification.

"This creature shall not know me. True enough it never saw me, but it was there at the salt mines in Afar, and it is here in the house of a councilor of the bala heg, and I do not like it. Maybe it can't hear, and maybe it can't speak, but it shall not know me—"

Anako held a tiny knife, a knife for peeling fruit, with a curved, pointed tip. He knelt by Telemakos's head, and bent over his face.

"Ugh, what a freak it is, it has the eyes of a dead thing! I should have insisted that idiot Scorpion let Dagale put its eyes out. But he would not spare me, not if he were offered the creature's weight in gold; so I must rid myself of it now, lest it denounce me—"

Telemakos lay watching the gold light struck off Anako's rings as the little dagger came closer to his eyes, and he could not lift one finger to protect himself.

He strained to move with all the force of his will. Anako hesitated, still chattering to himself, and Telemakos saw that Anako was frightened. Anako did not like to touch things. He had made Hara hurt Telemakos while he looked on. Suddenly Telemakos became so filled with hatred and disdain that there was no room in him for fear anymore.

"*Lazarus!*" Telemakos spat through his teeth. "I know you!"

Anako froze. The knife hesitated alongside Telemakos's cheekbone. Telemakos saw that he had bought himself an inch of space, a second of time.

"*I know you,*" he spat again. "How could I mistake you, Anako, governor of Deire? You smell like a baboon! Denounce you? I will lead you to the emperor myself! Lazarus! If you dare hurt me again, if you only dare *touch* me, my father will carve your living heart from your chest and eat it while it beats in his hands!"

Anako whispered, with both conviction and incredulity, "Harrier."

"Lazarus, call yourself Lazarus!" Telemakos blazed at him. "When have you ever had your face wound up in grave cloths? How long did you suffer your arms to be strapped fast as a corpse even while you lived? Who risked death to save your life? Jesus wept!"

Anako in desperation went for his throat. Telemakos in

desperation managed to twist his head aside, and Goewin's band of gold turned away the dagger. The little curved blade sank into his shoulder, and Telemakos shrieked as Anako wrenched it free.

Goewin was on top of them, battering Anako about the face with her fists and snatching for the knife. She cut her own hands on the blade, trying to get it away from him. Grandfather and the butler pulled them apart.

"Half a minute!" Goewin cried out. "Half a minute, he said! For God's sake, how long have you left them here alone? It is a trap, not a meeting of old friends, the child has offered himself up as a lure!"

There were others in the room as well, holding Anako back now. Turunesh lifted Telemakos's head and shoulders into her lap. Anako gasped, "Your serving thing attacked me—"

"Liar! Liar!" cried Telemakos. "Liar! I did nothing, I did not move or touch him, he was going to cut my throat! *Liar!*"

"Your serving thing—"

"Lij Telemakos is my grandson," said Grandfather dryly, "not my servant."

Then there was silence, but for the sound of Anako's quickening breaths as Ferem wrested the fruit knife from his hand, and Anako began to realize that he was caught.

Telemakos fought to find his limbs again. To move anything was like trying to swim through honey. Still his head did not hurt, but his shoulder throbbed and stabbed as his mother and aunt freed him from the folds of his shamma.

Goewin hissed when they discovered the wound.

"The murderous viper, look what he's *done* to the child! Medraut will never forgive me—" She shuddered. "Send for the court jeweler. He'll need to bring a small saw or something. I want this collar off. It's pressing against the wound when the child turns his head."

Telemakos gasped, "Oh, why can't I move!"

"Get this assassin out of my house," said Grandfather. "Take him to the stable yard and send to the New Palace for an escort of the imperial guard."

"Stop, wait!" Telemakos managed to get himself up on one knee. "*Wait*. Don't take him anywhere. I haven't finished; *I haven't finished*. Goewin, help me to stand."

He struggled up on her outstretched arms. His head was beginning to thump, now, which made him still more angry: Oh, the hardship I endured while this man grew rich, and the blinding fear and pain he dealt me! Telemakos held Goewin's elbow for support and advanced on his enemy.

Anako stood with his arms pinioned by the steward and the footman, not struggling, but hunching his head between his shoulders as though he could hide himself that way.

"Do you look at me, Anako," Telemakos commanded.

Anako looked down at the thin boy leaning on his aunt's arm, his clothes blood-soaked, bruises the size of doves' eggs rising over one eyebrow and aside the other. Anako looked, and looked away.

"I know my eyes scare you," Telemakos said coldly. "But the foreign blood that makes me seem such a freak to you also makes me a prince. I arrest you. I arrest you in the name of the emperor Gebre Meskal, king of Aksum and of all the tribes, the Beja, the Noba, the Kasu, and the Siyamo, Servant of the Cross. You stand accused of high treason against the Aksumite nation. The citizens of your ruined city anxiously await your arrival in the afterlife; I wish you joy of them."

Telemakos turned away from the one called the Lazarus, and said with satisfaction, "I have finished now."

He refused to be put to bed. He made Goewin and his mother help him out to the garden to wait for the jeweler, and for Medraut to see to his shoulder.

Turunesh stripped him of his stained shirt and shamma. "Good, the bleeding's stopped," she said calmly. "I'll get you clean clothes, love, and we'll wash that cut before your father gets here."

She went back inside. "Tell her to bring my book, too," Telemakos said to Goewin.

They made the mistake of leaving him alone for half a minute. Telemakos managed to drag himself over to the fish pond, so he could dabble in the water, and fell in up to his elbows.

"Telemakos!" His mother dropped the clothes she carried and ran to him. "You are your own worst enemy! You will drown yourself, or poison that wound! For pity's sake, stop trying to move!"

She settled him again. Goewin came back with his book.

"You are too excited to pay attention to this, I know,"

Turunesh said. "What can we do to distract you?"

Telemakos caught the animal scent again, the faint, sour smell that had betrayed Anako to him. He said suddenly, "I want to see the caracal."

"What a good idea."

Goewin went for the caracal. The tall boy that Telemakos had met by the well in the grove brought in the big black cat. Goewin paced at his side, apprehensive. They stopped before Telemakos.

The moustached boy held the creature's lead in both hands; but he let go one hand to scratch the cat between its ears. "Eh, Chariclea," the boy said fondly, and offered the lead to Telemakos. He glanced up at Goewin, and added quickly, "She won't pull."

"Thank you," Telemakos said. "What's your name?"

"Yesaka."

"I'm Telemakos."

"Lij Telemakos, she told me," the boy said, with another sidelong glance at Goewin.

"Well, yes. But no one bothers, usually, least of all my aunt. She's trying to scare you. Last time we met you thought I was someone's servant."

Yesaka said in a low voice, "That wasn't the last time we met."

The caracal sat down between them placidly and began to wash itself.

"What do you mean?"

"I saw you in Afar. When you were a prisoner there, when

you were brought before my master. I was there with him."

Goewin turned suddenly to Telemakos with narrowed eyes, vigilant and wary. Telemakos said cautiously, "Did you know who I was?"

"I guessed what you were. I knew the archon was looking for a spy, and I knew you were not what they took you for. I knew you were out of Gebre Meskal's court; I knew you could talk and hear, and that you must be blinding them to something."

"Did you say anything? Of course not, of course you didn't say anything, or I would no longer be alive." Telemakos was torn between wanting to know more about Anako's quietly rebellious animal keeper and the urgency of not allowing Goewin to know what had happened to him in Afar.

Curiosity won out over caution. "Why didn't you say anything?"

Yesaka suddenly knelt before Telemakos as he spoke. "If I kept silent, it meant I was an agent for the emperor as well. We were comrades, even if you did not know it. If I held silent, I was your conspirator, and neither one of us was alone."

"You were my comrade," Telemakos said quietly. "I did know it. I heard you weeping. It meant more to me than I can say."

The tall boy snatched at one of Telemakos's thin hands. He bent his head against it, and kissed it.

"I am your servant."

After Yesaka had been guided out of the garden court

again, Goewin knelt by Telemakos and pounded her fists together. "Now tell me truly, boy. *Why couldn't you see anything?*"

"I was blindfolded. Anako was afraid I would recognize him, and so I should have."

That did not sound so dreadful.

Goewin screwed up her mouth. "You are equivocating, I know it. Why was the caracal keeper weeping?"

That was nearly impossible to answer, but Telemakos plunged ahead anyway. "He couldn't keep it still, and they had to send him out. It scratched him, I think."

Telemakos bit his lip, and prayed that Goewin had not noticed the caracal's clawless feet.

ODYSSEUS BENDS HIS BOW

"No, I am your father—
the Odysseus you wept for all your days,
you bore a world of pain, the cruel abuse of men."
16:212–14

TELEMAKOS LAY ALONG the edge of the big fountain in the Golden Court, trailing his fingers in the water. The sound of the fountains was making him sleepy. The air smelled moist and warm, of palm and aloe. He was watching the fish.

"Your shamma's getting wet," Sofya said.

She sat down on the floor by the fountain's marble lip. "What are you doing in here? I thought you were at the trial."

"They're in recess. It is the sentencing next."

"I wish they might let me in," Sofya said. "But well we know it is no place for an owlish little girl."

"No one thinks you're stupid."

"All do."

"Gebre Meskal doesn't. Nor does my aunt. Nobody else matters." Telemakos spoke to the fish. "You're right, though:

there is no place in this trial for little girls. I wish there was no place for me, either. I hate it. I feel so sorry for Karkara; I know what he's done, but still I pity him. I do not like to see him led about in chains. And Anako—"

Anako never said anything, but he oozed hatred at Telemakos. He stared and sneered as though Telemakos were a leper.

"I wish I had played I was still sick, so Gebre Meskal would not make me sit through it." Telemakos sat up, and tried to wring out the damp end of his shamma. "It makes me tired."

"Everything makes you tired," Sofya said.

"I have to go back now." Telemakos picked up the linen head cloth that lay at his feet and carefully unfolded it.

"What is that?"

"You've never seen me dressed in anything but rags, or pondweed, have you? Your mother gave me this to wear, this mantle." He had folded it inside the head cloth; it was a collar of filigreed gold and emerald that lay over the shoulders of his shamma. It was splendid to look on and weighed on him more heavily than had the ring of gold he no longer wore. It rubbed brutally at the stitches in his upper arm.

Telemakos carefully lifted the mantle over his shoulders and banded the head cloth in place. It did not hide the matching black bruises on either side of his forehead, where Anako had struck him.

"You would look quite grown up, if you were taller," said Sofya.

"I look like a pirate."

"You look like a prince who has been to battle."

This was undoubtedly the most complimentary thing she had ever said to him, and it gave Telemakos again that strange feeling of faint sadness, such as he had felt watching Sofya adorn Esato as a bride.

"The last person to wear this necklet was your brother Hector," Telemakos said. "It was your father's."

"I don't remember Hector. He died when we were very little, Esato and I. I remember my brother Priamos weeping for Hector, though, after the war in Himyar. My brothers and sisters are all so *old*, except Esato. I am alone, now."

"Well," said Telemakos, "I have always been alone, and it is not so terrible. You can share my new sister, when she comes, if you like."

"It might be a brother."

"She will be a sister. But you can share her anyway." Telemakos stood up. "I have to go. I might come back another time."

"I might be here," said Sofya.

Telemakos took his place again in the courtroom, between his father and his aunt. Goewin was the only woman of the company, a thing that must be usual to her. What could it feel like, to be so alien all the time?

She reached across to clasp Telemakos's hand. All through the tedious opening formalities she sat staring down at his torn fingernails, one of them yellowed and peeling, the other growing in new and crooked over soft raw skin. Telemakos sat upright and formal, weighted by his adult finery. He gazed directly ahead of him, frowning as Karkara bowed to him politely and made him feel a Judas. Then Anako came past Telemakos, and spat in his face.

Telemakos winced involuntarily, as though Anako's venom were real, and burned.

The emperor's guards held Medraut down in his seat. There was no other sound in the hall, but for this wordless struggle. Gebre Meskal broke into the silence, speaking low and level. "Lij Telemakos, perhaps you would like to pass sentence on this man Anako yourself?"

"I, Your Majesty?"

"If you wish."

Telemakos stood in his place and freed his hand from Goewin's clasp. "I would like to wash my face first," he said.

A page of his own age brought him a tray and a bowl, and Telemakos carefully dipped his hand in the water and wiped his fingers back across his cheek.

"Thank you, Your Majesty."

"I pray you, Lij Telemakos, pass your sentence now."

"I do not know how it should be spoken."

"Never mind the formula. Simply tell me how you would punish this man, if he were in your hands. Tell me anything you wish. You have earned this right."

Telemakos trailed his fingers in the bowl of water at his side. He said at last, "Send him to Afar."

"To toil in the salt he loves so dearly?" the emperor prompted. "Yes. Go on."

"Send him to Afar," Telemakos repeated slowly. "Let him be blindfolded, and bound with his hands at his sides so he can't take off the blindfold, and let his eyes be rubbed with grease mixed with gravel to glue them shut. Then let him spend his days bearing water to the salt cutters. Let him start each day carrying half his weight in water, always bound and blinded; and feed him nothing but stale injera; and though he brings water to all the other men there, let him be given no more than the twentieth part of a single skin in a day. And if he stumbles in his work let his hands be strapped behind him and have him lashed. But if he complains or weeps aloud or makes any kind of noise, ever, if he so much as voices a sigh or a cough, *ever*, then for each word or groan, take off one of his fingernails with a knife—"

His own words made him flinch. The bowl at his fingertips went flying off the tray and shattered on the floor in a mess of clay and water.

Anako stammered, "Mercy demands—"

The emperor cut him short. "This would be a slow and cruel death," said Gebre Meskal quietly. "He may survive a week on such a regime, but so little of a skin is not sufficient water for a man laboring in the desert."

Telemakos said through his teeth, "*It is for a child.*"

A gasp at his back made Telemakos look behind him. His grandfather, and Ityopis of the bala heg, and two of the pages, and even Karkara, were all weeping shamelessly. His aunt was bent double with her head caught and hidden in her arms, pulling at her hair with taut fingers, her whole body shaking.

Telemakos stood appalled at his own carelessness. He had given himself away.

His father did not weep. He stood up and rapped Goewin on the back of her head with the edge of his hand. Medraut spoke to her hoarsely, but aloud:

"So your brother is avenged."

Nearly every head in the hall turned to stare at Medraut in thunderstruck astonishment. Even the emperor stared at him.

Only Goewin did not. She sobbed gaspingly, her head still clutched in her arms. Telemakos felt all his poise slipping away. He had known how cruelly this would hurt Goewin.

"You vengeful harridan," said Medraut coldly.

Goewin cried out as though in pain, as though there were a knife between her ribs.

"Telemakos—Telemakos, forgive me, I never knew—I knew you suffered, but you would not say—you never spoke of this—"

Medraut looked down at her wrathfully. The hard hand with which he had struck her was poised over her bent neck, as though he meant to strike her again but could not bring himself to touch so contemptible a creature a second time.

Telemakos stormed at his father in fury, "Goewin is crying for *me*. You are wallowing in guilt for what you did five years ago to your dead brother. How can you be so selfish, so blind? You cannot heap all the burden of blame on Goewin's shoulders! It was my decision to go to Afar, *my own;* and but for your lousy leaking water bag I should not have had to surrender myself!"

Then Medraut's head sank and his shoulders slumped as though he had been dealt a mortal wound, and Telemakos faltered. He tried to explain. "I mean, we are all in it together. None of us is innocent; none of us is alone."

Medraut spoke heavily, in a hoarse whisper:

"You were both."

The emperor's voice rang with warning, sharp and deadly even: "You have not been given leave to speak, Ras Meder."

The words seemed to hang echoing throughout the hall for a long, frozen moment. The emperor rebuked Medraut again in the same chill, level voice, saying simply, "'Physician, heal yourself.'"

Medraut fell back into his seat by his sister. Now they were bent double side by side, both with their faces in their hands, while Telemakos stood helplessly between them with no idea what to do or say next.

"Lij Telemakos," continued Gebre Meskal calmly, "this court remains in session. I have asked you to suggest a sentence for this criminal. Have you given it?"

"I have. I—" Telemakos said, and clenched his fists. He hated Anako, but he did not want to be like Anako. "I have not. Plague take him! Send him into exile outside Aksum. Give him a choice: Afar or exile. Salt or plague. Maybe he will be lucky."

Telemakos stopped, and sighed. The emperor turned to

the cringing Anako, who at this attention prostrated himself at Gebre Meskal's feet. Karkara had not stopped weeping.

"This is a formal trial of the Aksumite Empire, not a house of mourning or confessional," Gebre Meskal stated, his voice still dangerously controlled. "Lij Telemakos, escort your father and the British ambassador to a place where they may better compose themselves. We will proceed without you."

Telemakos offered his arm to Goewin. She took it, and let him lead her, shielding her eyes with her other hand and shaking still with choking sobs. Medraut bowed to the emperor and followed them out.

Telemakos went where he always went for solace, straight to Solomon and Sheba.

The keeper was there. Telemakos led Goewin to the little garden of tall, bright flame flowers above the lion pit, and made her sit on the stone bench set against the railing. He called down to the keeper. "Nezana, can we have Solomon up here?"

"Is that you, Telemakos?"

"Is there another who comes along asking to play with your lions?"

"Who's with you?"

"My father and my aunt."

"Yes, all right. Let me muzzle him, and I'll bring him through the tunnel to you."

Telemakos knelt on the bench beside Goewin, his arms around her neck, and kissed her face. Medraut leaned over the railing, watching as the keeper woke Solomon.

"I'll be only seconds," Telemakos said, and ran down the flagged steps to the tunnel's entrance.

Solomon buffeted his enormous gold and black head against Telemakos's chest, nearly knocking him over. Nezana let go of the great lion's harness.

"Stupid muzzle," Telemakos said softly, scratching his friend with both hands behind the lion's ears.

"He could still flatten you with one paw," Nezana said, shaking his head.

"You know he won't. Come up, Solomon, come and meet my family."

Telemakos climbed back to the garden, the lion pressing its head at his side as he made his way up the narrow steps. Goewin raised her tearstained face as Telemakos came near, and Medraut also turned to look at him.

"Oh, Telemakos, what are you, *what are you?*" Goewin whispered.

"What am I?" Telemakos frowned. "What do you mean?"

"Look at you, look at you! You are so young and so slight, and you stand unafraid with your arm around a lion's neck!"

Telemakos glanced down at his arm. Sunlight caught at the emeralds spread over his shoulders, and dazzled him. He looked up again.

"Solomon is my friend. He's tame. He'd eat me, otherwise."

Telemakos brought Solomon to sit at Goewin's feet.

"Here, stroke his mane, Goewin," Telemakos said. "He's such a softy. Not a proper lion at all. You wouldn't last a day in the wilderness, would you, lazy old Solomon? Oh, Goewin, please don't cry anymore."

"How long were you blindfolded?" she whispered.

"Goewin, please don't."

"How long?"

He saw that to leave her to guess was worse torment than to tell her the truth.

"Two months, I think."

"Did he torture you himself?"

Telemakos did not answer. Goewin reached over to touch his fingertips. "Did Anako do this?"

He would not tell her.

"Make an answer," Medraut scolded his son, in his dark, beautiful voice. It was the first he had spoken since leaving the court. When Telemakos still hesitated, Medraut added: "I bid you."

He waited.

"I bid you, Telemakos," Medraut ruled quietly.

Telemakos was undone. His resolve disintegrated at the sound of his father's voice speaking his name.

"Anako didn't do it himself. Another used his knife, to his command."

"Why?" Goewin whispered.

"To see if I could talk."

"Ah, God." Goewin closed her eyes and swallowed hard, and sank her head in her arms again. "Ah, God forgive me."

The lion tried to settle its great bulk against her knee.

Goewin raised her head and laid one trembling hand on Solomon's heavy black mane.

"But you bore it in silence," she whispered. "Until that night in Kidane's house Anako thought you were mute. So you never cried out, you never made a sound. *What kind of being are you?*"

On the other side of the little garden, a tiny, shining bird with iridescent emerald wings darted among the tall red flowers. Telemakos pointed. "There."

Goewin shook her head in disbelief and said chokingly, with the faintest of smiles, "Sunbird."

Telemakos laughed. "You have said so."

Medraut sat down at Goewin's side and took her in his arms. "All right, little sister," he said, in that low, quiet, musical voice, stroking her hair. "All right."

"I did not mean to hurt him—" Goewin gasped.

"He is right. We were all in it together, striving to deliver the nation."

"So we have," she muttered fiercely. "Or anyway most of it."

"So we have," Medraut said. Suddenly he buried his face in his sister's shoulder with a sob. "Oh, that my child should be so misused, my only child—It feels like vengeance, a justice against me—" He gave another agonized sob. "God forgive us both."

Medraut was talking. Medraut was speaking aloud, in conversation, awake.

"I'm not your only child," said Telemakos.

Medraut stretched one arm open to include his son in his embrace.

"I was so lonely," Telemakos said. "The worst thing about it was the loneliness." He looked up at his father, at the tears streaking Medraut's hard, lined face. "Not ever being spoken to. There was nothing more terrible. It was worse than dying of thirst."

"You put us all to shame, little one," Medraut said.

This was worth more than all the salt in Afar, more than all Sasu's gold. This was worth everything.

Telemakos kissed his father's cheek, unable to contain his delight. Medraut sighed, and smiled faintly at his son with the quirking corner of his mouth.

"Come, Telemakos," he said. "You've finished your task for the emperor. Will you come home with me now?" He hesitated, searching for words so long untried. "Put your lion away, and let us all go home, and I shall read to you from your *Telemakia*."

It had all been worth this.

FAMILY TREE

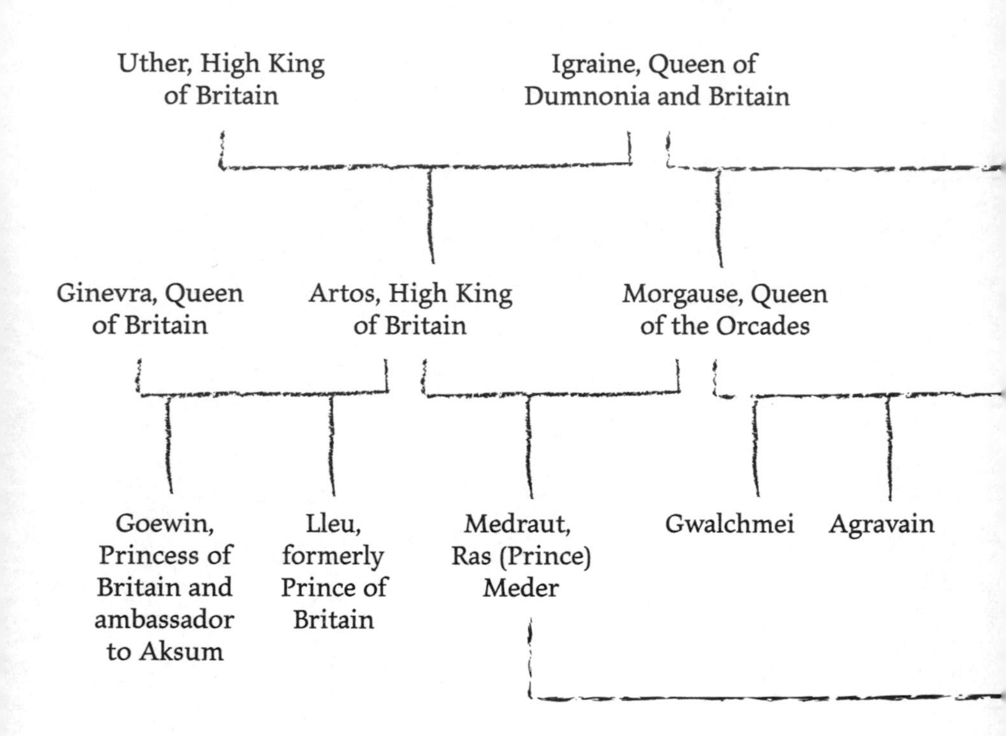

Uther, High King of Britain
Igraine, Queen of Dumnonia and Britain
Ginevra, Queen of Britain
Artos, High King of Britain
Morgause, Queen of the Orcades
Goewin, Princess of Britain and ambassador to Aksum
Lleu, formerly Prince of Britain
Medraut, Ras (Prince) Meder
Gwalchmei
Agravain

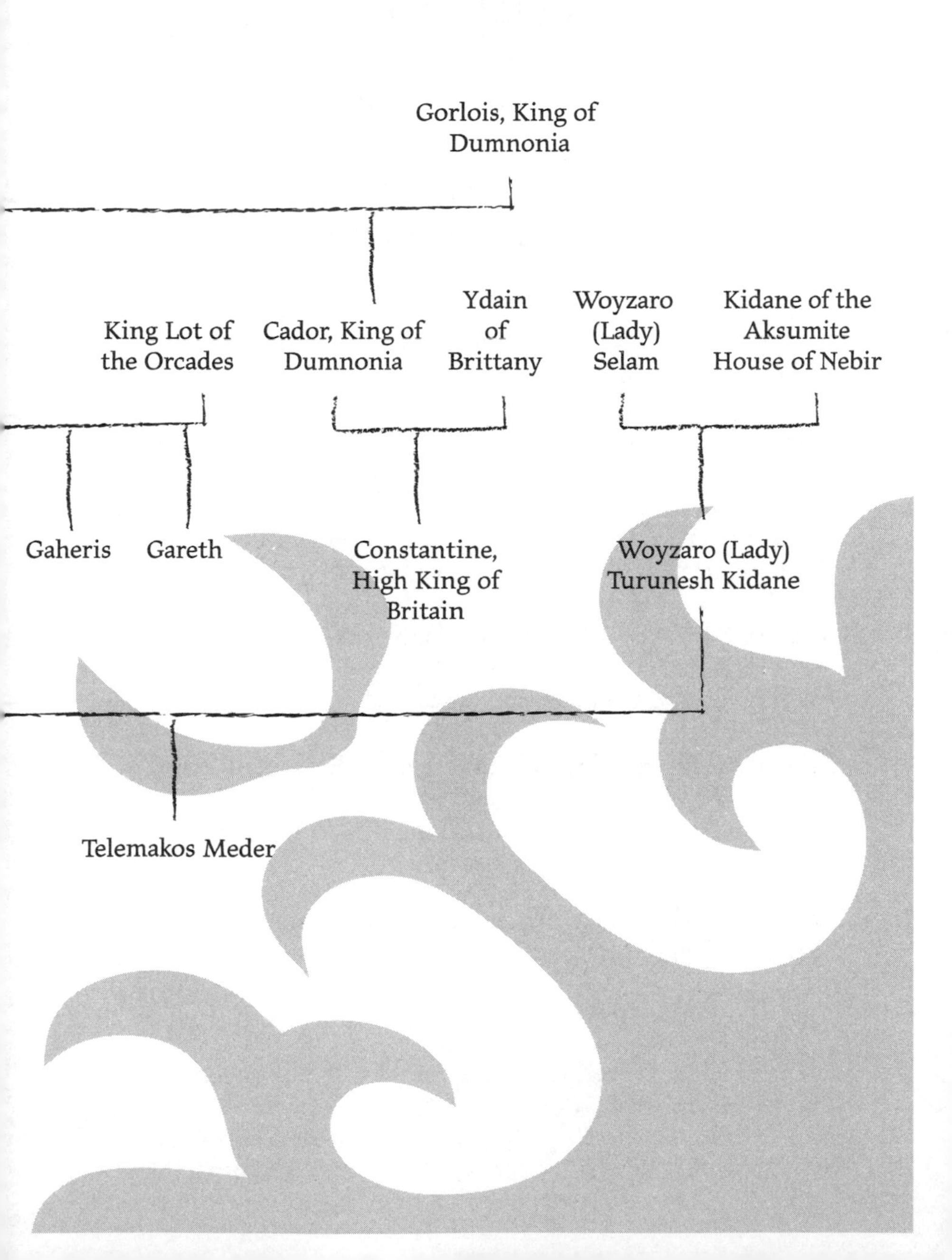

Gorlois, King of Dumnonia
King Lot of the Orcades
Cador, King of Dumnonia
Ydain of Brittany
Woyzaro (Lady) Selam
Kidane of the Aksumite House of Nebir
Gaheris
Gareth
Constantine, High King of Britain
Woyzaro (Lady) Turunesh Kidane
Telemakos Meder

GLOSSARY

G=Ge'ez, or ancient Ethiopic
A=Amharic, or modern Ethiopian

ABUNA (**A**): Bishop.

AGABE HEG (**G**): Spokesman for the emperor's parliament, and closest advisor to the emperor.

AMOLE (**A**): Block of salt, used as currency in parts of Ethiopia from ancient times through to the present day.

BALA HEG (**G**): Parliament of advisors to the emperor.

BLATTE (**A**): Councilor.

INJERA (**A**): Flat bread made from tef, Ethiopian grain.

LIJ (**A**): Title for a young prince (similar to European "childe").

MESOB (**A**): Large covered basket that doubles as a table; used for storing injera.

NEBIR (**A**): Leopard.

NEGESHTA NAGASHTAT (**G**): Queen of queens (here, the emperor's aunt).

NEGUS (**G**, **A**): King.

NEGUSA NAGAST (**G**): Emperor (literally "king of kings").

RAS (**A**): Title for a duke or prince.

SANTARAJ (**A**): Ethiopian chess.

SHAMMA (**A**): Cotton shawl worn over clothes by men and women.

TEF (**A**): Endemic Ethiopian grain, used to make flour.

WAIDELLA (**Afar**): Cairn built as a monument to the dead.

WAT (**A**): Stew made from meat, vegetables, beans, lentils, etc.

WOYZARO (**A**): Noble lady or princess.

ELIZABETH E. WEIN was born in New York City and grew up in England, Jamaica, and Pennsylvania. She has a B.A. from Yale and a Ph.D. from the University of Pennsylvania.

She has written two other novels in her ongoing Arthurian/Aksumite cycle: *The Winter Prince* and *A Coalition of Lions*.

Elizabeth and her husband both ring church bells in the English style known as "change ringing." They also fly small planes. They live in Scotland with their two young children.